700034971037

SHERLOCK HOLMES
AND THE
AMERICAN ANGELS

*Sherlock Holmes titles by Barrie Roberts
available from Severn House Large Print*

Sherlock Holmes and the Rule of Nine
Sherlock Holmes and the King's Governess

SHERLOCK HOLMES AND THE AMERICAN ANGELS

A manuscript believed to be from the pen of

John H. Watson

Annotated and edited by Barrie Roberts

Severn House Large Print
London & New York

SEVERN HOUSE PUBLISHERS of
9-15 High Street, Sutton, Surrey, SM1 1DF.
First world regular print edition published 2007 by
Severn House Publishers, London and New York.

British Library Cataloguing in Publication Data

Roberts, Barrie, 1939-
 Sherlock Holmes and the American Angels : a manuscript
 believed to be from the pen of John H. Watson. - Large
 print ed.
 1. Holmes, Sherlock (Fictitious character) - Fiction
 2. Watson, John H. (Fictitious character) - Fiction
 3. Scotland - Antiquities - Fiction 4. Detective and
 mystery stories 5. Large type books
 I. Title
 823.9'14[F]

ISBN-13: 978-0-7278-7706-2

Printed and bound in Great Britain by
MPG Books Ltd, Bodmin, Cornwall.

Editor's Note

The text presented here derives from one of a number of manuscripts which have been in the possession of my family for some years. I cannot be certain of their origin, but my maternal grandfather was both a medical man and a contemporary of Dr Watson in the RAMC during the Great War. I have edited nine of those manuscripts for book publication: *Sherlock Holmes and the Railway Maniac* (Constable, 1994*), Sherlock Holmes and the Devil's Grail* (Constable, 1995*), Sherlock Holmes and the Man from Hell* (Constable, 1997), *Sherlock Holmes and the Royal Flush* (Constable, 1998), 'The Mystery of the Addleton Curse', which appeared in *The Mammoth Book of New Sherlock Holmes Adventures* (Robinson Books, 1998), *Sherlock Holmes and the Harvest of Death* (Constable, 1999), *Sherlock Holmes and the Crosby Murder,* (Constable, 2000), *Sherlock Holmes and the Rule of Nine* (Severn House, 2002), and *Sherlock Holmes and the King's Governess* (Severn House, 2005). In addition, some of the shorter manuscripts I have edited for the *Strand Magazine* in the USA.

I have, as always, sought proof that this is a genuine record by Dr John H. Watson of a previously unknown case of Sherlock Holmes, but to establish absolute provenance is almost impossible, partly because there is no unimpeachable specimen of Watson's handwriting available, apart from his habit of fictionalizing names and places.

At the end of the book will be found my notes on my research into some aspects of the story. With what little help these give, the reader must make up their own mind as to whether this really is a previously unknown adventure of the Great Detective. Personally, I am as satisfied as reason permits.

Barrie Roberts
December 2006

Personal Messages

In my present attempt to chronicle as completely as my notes, my memory and a proper discretion will permit, the many enquiries undertaken by my friend Mr Sherlock Holmes during our partnership, together with what I know of his cases before and after that period, I have often had to pause and consider whether I dare commit to paper, let alone publish, the facts in some of his cases.

I have usually assuaged my conscience by concealing the identities of participants in a case, or altering trivial details, so that no positive confirmation of individuals or events can be made. In a small number of cases, the real events on which matters turned were so consequential that they could not reasonably be disguised. One such was the curious case which I have previously referred to as 'the services which may some day be described'* without revealing

*See *The Adventure of The Three Garridebs* by Sir Arthur Conan Doyle.

7

in whose interest Holmes provided those services.

For the reasons which I have set out, it is with no little trepidation that I pen this account of the affair of the American angels. Where I can conceal identities I have done so, but there are certain historical realities involved with which I cannot tamper. The affair was of the utmost importance to the United States, which seemed threatened by serious public disorder if not a second civil war, while it posed at very least the possibility of grave embarrassment to Britain and France. The story could not be told at the time without, perhaps, provoking the very results which were feared, but it is wrong that it should slip from the record of history. I have made no arrangement for the publication of these later records of Holmes' cases, only for their preservation. It may be that they may be published harmlessly in years to come and serve only to fill in a blank area of English, American and Scottish history.

My journal shows that the affair began in a seemingly trivial fashion in the spring of 1902. I came down to breakfast one morning to find Holmes ahead of me at the table. He was dressed in the mouse-coloured dressing gown which was one of only two I had ever seen him wear in the two decades of our friendship and which was, I have to remark, growing decidedly threadbare. The usual drift of the morning newspapers covered the table and a large part of the floor.

As I poked about among the papers looking for the toast I noticed that Holmes was paying close attention to an item in one paper and copying something into his pocketbook. I located the toast rack and Mrs Hudson arrived with my breakfast and a fresh pot of tea.

While I took my meal Holmes was almost entirely uncommunicative, replying to my attempts at conversation with meaningless grunts, while his eyes moved only between the newspaper and the jottings he was making in his pocketbook.

At last I put aside my napkin, poured myself another cup of tea and asked, 'What are you doing, Holmes?'

He looked up. 'I am,' he said, 'deciphering a series of personal messages which I have noted in the newspapers over the last few days.'

I smiled. 'Really, Holmes, I have never understood your delight in unravelling messages which are usually the product of illicit romantic arrangements which are nobody else's business, or complicated commercial messages unintelligible to an outsider.'

'In the main, Watson, you are right, but sometimes the cryptic advertisers are driven by impulses other than the whimsy of love or the pressures of commerce. Here and there among the dross you mention there are occasional gems, and I believe that I have hit upon one.'

'Oh, really?' I said, with a trace of scorn. 'And what great crime is revealed in these messages?'

'I do not know,' admitted Holmes, 'but there are features of these advertisements that suggest their purpose, whatever it may be, is neither romantic nor commercial. See what you think, Watson.'

He passed me four newspaper cuttings, which he had marked with their dates of publication. The first had appeared a few days previously and read:

'BENJAMIN – HYEVH V?AEO RCIET EEIEV UEDDC'

The first was sufficient to discourage me and I barely glanced at the other three except to note that they were broadly similar.

'You know very well that I have no head for codes,' I protested. 'All I can see is that all five words have five letters.'

'Groups, not words,' Holmes corrected me. 'I have explained to you before, Watson, that it is the usual practise of those who use ciphers to write their messages in groups of the same size. It serves to conceal the structure of the text.'

'How does that help?' I asked.

'Perhaps not very much at this stage, but what does help is the question mark,' said Holmes. 'Assuming, since it appeared in a London newspaper, that the message is in English, I wondered if the advertiser had made the serious mistake of ending an interrogative message with a question mark.'

'Why is that a serious mistake?'

'It is a very grave error, Watson, because it reveals the end of the message and a part of its purpose and thereby suggests the word or words with which the message may commence.'

'I can see,' I said, 'that it reveals the end of the text and also makes clear that it is a question, but I don't understand how it reveals the beginning.'

'It is a question of twenty-five letters. In English such a phrase is likely to begin with one of a small number of expressions such as "have you", "will you", "can you" and so on.'

I looked at the message again. 'I can see that "have you" might well be there, but if it is it has been well and truly jumbled up. How can it be sorted out?'

'Excellent, Watson! You are doing very well! However, a cipher must be intelligible to at least two parties, so it can only be jumbled according to a pattern which both understand. Once again, the question mark suggests an element of that pattern. Instead of being at the end of the text, it lies one third in, which suggested to me that the message had been sliced into three in some way.'

He paused and felt in his pockets for his pipe.

'Now,' he continued, 'there are many ways in which you can jumble a message into three unintelligible parts. For example, you might write "the cat sat on the mat" in vertical columns of three letters. Having done so, reading across the columns, instead of down them, would give you TCSOHA, HAANET, ETTTM – three apparently meaningless groups of letters.'

'But that,' I said, 'gives away the T, the H and the E at the beginning of each group, and might lead someone to discover the message.'

'You excel yourself, Watson!' he exclaimed. 'That is exactly right. To prevent discovery, something else has to be done.'

He had filled his pipe and now lit it, drawing contentedly for a moment before he continued.

'In considering that aspect of the problem,' he went on, 'it occurred to me that there is an American cipher system known as a "rail fence" cipher, which might be used to split a text into three parts.'

'A rail fence!' I exclaimed.

'So called,' said Holmes, 'because, when written out for encipherment, the message resembles one of those zigzag wooden fences that are common in many parts of America. Look!'

He passed me his pocketbook, opened at a page on which he had written the message in a zigzag pattern. It read:

BENJAMIN –
H Y E V H V ?
A E O R C I E T E E I E
V U E D D C

'By reordering the text so,' continued my friend, 'and further reordering it by reading across the horizontal lines, you come to the message as published: "Have you received the device?".'

I nodded. 'What is the device mentioned?' I asked.

'I wish I knew,' said Holmes. 'The day after that message appeared it was followed by the second advertisement. Have a look at it.'

I picked up the second cutting. It read:

CHARLES – DCCEE PIURE IEEEV
DLAEU LSNME OVRIP SBHBO

'Is it in the same code?' I enquired.

Holmes nodded. 'Have a go at it,' he suggested, and passed me a piece of paper and his mechanical pencil.

I looked at the message and then asked, 'But where do I begin?'

'Try the fact that this is an answer to the first message and probably contains the word "device",' suggested Holmes.

It still took me several attempts before, with considerable assistance from Holmes, I managed to construct the following:

D C C E E P I U R
E I E E E V D L A E U L S N M E O
V R I P S B H B O

'"Device received, please publish number",' I read from it. 'Well, it is clearly a reply to the first message.'

Holmes nodded. 'What about the third?' he asked.

I examined the news cutting. 'Hold hard, Holmes,' I said. 'This isn't to either of the first two advertisers. This is to someone called Franklin.'

Holmes made an impatient grimace. 'Watson,' he said, 'do you not think that the Franklin of the third message may also be the Benjamin of the first?'

I stared at him for a moment before I made the connection. 'Of course!' I exclaimed. 'Benjamin Franklin! Then you think these are Americans?'

'One of them may be,' said Holmes, 'but they seem to be more than that. Now try the message.'

I looked at it again. It ran:

FRANKLIN – NE:RF TEOUB RMH(E)
3554 500SI2 DSF00

'It's more complicated,' I said. 'It has numbers and symbols in it.'

'So far,' said Holmes, 'they have used the rail fence trick twice. In this instance they used it again. I suggest you try the word "number".'

It took yet more of my friend's hints before I finally achieved this:

```
N  E  :  R  F  T  E  0
U  B  R  S  H  (E)  3  5  5  4  5  0  0
M  I  2  D  S  L  0  0
```

I succeeded in extracting a message of a kind:

'It makes no sense to me,' I admitted.

'Nor to me,' agreed Holmes, 'but it evidently made sense to the respondent, because he immediately set a meeting in hand. Look at the last message.'

The last message was much longer than its predecessors. It said:

STUART – NEDTWB BHHCE- UBRNES ODILEN ECRGTF GTR2MU ROLONI OAP

I laboured at it for a while before admitting defeat.

'Watson!' chided Holmes. 'It is the same cipher as before. It is merely longer.'

He showed me his note of the message written out zigzag fashion:

N E D T W B B H H C E -
U B R N E S O D I L E N E C R
G T F G T R 2
  M U R O L O N I O A P

I managed to read it out.

'"Number understood, will be on bench right of C Gate RP 2 -". What on earth can that mean?' I asked. 'We now have four people exchanging coded messages of increasing obscurity! I can make nothing of it all!'

'Two persons only,' corrected Holmes. 'The use of a different name on each message is merely a device to deflect the eye of the casual observer. I suspect there are only two correspondents, an American and a Scot.'

I looked up at him, startled. 'How do you deduce that from these messages, Holmes?'

He smiled. 'One is addressed as "Benjamin" and "Franklin"; the other is addressed as "Charles" and "Stuart". I would think it extremely unlikely that pure chance led them to use the names of a prominent American and a prominent Scot.'

I nodded. 'But why an American and a Scot?' I asked.

'The answer to that may lie in other connections between the parties,' said Holmes. 'I think you will now agree, Watson, that this correspondence is not between furtive lovers, and it does not seem to be a commercial matter. Perhaps you will forgive me if I say that I detect the smell of an illicit conspiracy.'

'You may well be right,' I said. 'They are evidently not lovers, but what kind of conspiracy do you have in mind? What "other connections" do you detect between the parties?'

'That the noms de plume which they have chosen are not only those of a prominent American and a prominent Scot, Watson, but those of two prominent Jacobites.'

'Jacobites!' I protested. 'Really, Holmes! Surely the Jacobite cause was finally defeated in the 1745 rebellion?'

'The rebels were defeated in the field,' agreed my friend, 'but that does not mean the cause was destroyed. There are still many who believe that the Stuarts are the rightful monarchs of Britain.'

'Holmes!' I expostulated. 'There are times when I believe that you take your theories a deal too far. The Jacobite cause died at Culloden, a century and a half ago. While I grant you that these messages are evidently about some illegal enterprise, it is impossible to believe that they herald a new Jacobite rebellion!'

'We shall see, Watson, we shall see,' he said mildly.

'How shall we see?' I asked, with some sharpness.

'Because they have made an appointment to meet,' he said, 'and by chance they have set it in our immediate vicinity. You are always recommending a little exercise after meals, Watson. Perhaps you would care to join me for a stroll in Regent's Park after luncheon?'

'Regent's Park?' I queried. 'Is that where they are meeting?'

'I imagine that "C gate RP 2" in the last message means the Clarence Gate of Regent's Park at two o'clock. What else? I propose that we forestall them and get at least a glimpse of our conspirators.'

So it was that, after our luncheon, Holmes and I strolled up Baker Street and entered the park by the Clarence Gate.

It was early in the afternoon of a weekday and there were few people in the park, most of them at some distance. Indeed, I had thought the area immediately adjacent to the Clarence Gate to be deserted until I became aware of a man seated with his back to us on a bench to the right of the gate.

The figure wore a wide-brimmed straw hat and a linen coat. At first I believed that a red scarf was wound about his neck, beneath his red hair, then I realized with horror that the red colour on the back of his coat was blood, pouring from a wound in the neck.

I sprang across to the bench, closely followed by Holmes. It took but a moment to determine that the man was dead, having been stabbed deeply in the back of the neck with a small horn-handled knife.

'This poor fellow is beyond my help,' I said to Holmes as I straightened up.

Holmes was looking about him. 'His assailant,' he said, 'seems to have got clean away.' He pointed with his stick. 'Run down to the Marylebone Road, Watson, and see if there is a constable by Tussauds while I keep guard here.'

Sherlock Holmes Deduces

I made my best speed down Baker Street and was fortunate, on arriving at Marylebone Road, to find a uniformed sergeant and a constable there. Sending the constable for reinforcements, the sergeant accompanied me back to the park.

Holmes stood near the bench, gazing about him keenly, and I recall reflecting that he did not seem at all put out by having discovered a murdered man in the park.

'Good afternoon, Sergeant,' he said. 'Dr Watson will have explained to you that we came across this unfortunate fellow while walking off our lunch. We did not see the perpetrator, but he cannot have escaped long before our arrival on the scene. I think he went in that direction,' he said, pointing across the park with his stick. 'Had he left by the Clarence Gate I believe we should have seen him.'

I had imagined that Holmes would wish to wait until a detective arrived, but he gave his card to the sergeant, told him that we would await his superiors at Baker Street, and wished him good afternoon.

It was not until we were back in our rooms that I asked him, 'Why did we not wait for a detective, Holmes?'

'There is little, I suspect, that any denizen of Scotland Yard could tell me about the victim or the murderer. I took the opportunity of your absence to make a few fundamental examinations of my own.'

I waited expectantly for him to recite his observations and deductions, but he was in that self-satisfied mood which seized him often when he simply ignored my curiosity.

'You are quite right, Watson,' he remarked. 'Exercise after luncheon does have beneficial results. Would you ring for Mrs Hudson and suggest some tea and scones?'

He was on his second cup of tea and had done more than justice to a plate of scones when Mrs Hudson returned to tell him that Inspector Hopkins from Scotland Yard was below.

Holmes sprang from his chair as the detective entered and shook the Scotland Yarder warmly by the hand.

'Stanley Hopkins!' he exclaimed. 'I hope that this means you are put in charge of the Regent's Park murder. We have seen too little of you lately and you've never brought us a dull case yet.'

He ushered Hopkins to a chair, calling for more tea and scones as he did so.

'Well, Mr Holmes,' said Hopkins, once he was seated, 'Some of us have made it a practise to call upon you when we were perplexed by a case, but I have to say that we have made a little progress in persuading the Yard to adopt some of your thinking, so we are not so often perplexed.

'However, I haven't come to take your advice, welcome as it always is, but to see you as an important witness to the Regent's Park matter.'

'If not as a suspect!' commented Holmes, with a raised eyebrow.

'Oh, indeed,' agreed Hopkins, with a straight face. 'Though I suspect that I can ignore that possibility.'

He drew out his pocketbook and thumbed through its pages.

'Can I begin,' he said, 'with something you said to my sergeant? After you'd left he thought it peculiar and repeated it to me. He claims that you said the murderer probably escaped across the park, because if he'd used the Clarence Gate you would have seen him. Did you say that, Mr Holmes?'

'I did.'

'And does that mean that you know the perpetrator?'

'No, Hopkins, but I know certain things

about him. I know that he is tall and muscular, that he limps with his left leg and that he is almost certainly Scottish. The flow of blood showed me that the victim had been dead only a very short time when Watson and I entered the park. If the killer had left by the Clarence Gate we would have passed him as we arrived from Baker Street but we saw no such person.'

After twenty years, Holmes' ability to make accurate deductions from small facts still amazed me, and now Hopkins stared at him.

'If you do not know the man,' he said, 'how can you say so much about him, Mr Holmes?'

'Because you were curious about my comment to the sergeant, Hopkins, you commenced your inquiry with the wrong question. Let me begin at the beginning,' said Holmes.

At this point Mrs Hudson arrived with fresh tea and a further plate of scones. When we were all served, Holmes began his recital.

'After our luncheon,' he said, throwing me a warning glance, 'Watson prevailed upon me to take a stroll in the park. That was at a little before two. We walked up this side of Baker Street and crossed over to the park gate. We had hardly stepped into the park before we became aware of a man seated on the bench close to the gate and that he was injured. Once Watson had confirmed that the man was beyond assistance, he set out to find a police officer. That much you know, Inspector. Now let me give you the fruits of the examinations I made in Watson's absence.'

He paused to butter yet another scone, a clear indication that he was enjoying himself, then continued.

'What do you know of the murder weapon?' he asked.

'It hasn't been removed from the victim's neck,' said Hopkins, 'but from what can be seen of it I would say that it is a fairly small weapon with a handle of some kind of dark wood, at the base of which is a decorative silver ring enclosing some sort of semi-precious stone. It was driven into the victim's neck with some force.'

Holmes nodded. 'You are correct as to the weapon, Hopkins. It is a skean-dhu. The name is Scots Gaelic, and means "black knife". It is so called both because of the handle, which is of black bog oak, and the purpose which it served. It could be readily concealed among the owner's clothing, and so serve as an unpleasant surprise to his enemy. It is, in fact, designed for forceful stabbing at close quarters.'

'Which is what we have here,' said Hopkins.

Holmes shook his head. 'No, we do not,' he said. 'Although the weapon is devised with the quick stab in mind, that is not how our victim died.'

'It certainly looked like it to me, Holmes,' I protested. 'A single forceful blow, angled slightly upwards so as to enter the base of the brain. It was an assassin's blow – it will have killed his victim instantly with no outcry.'

'That might have been so if the victim was sitting upright,' conceded my friend, 'but he was not. Hopkins will confirm that he had his pocket watch in his left hand. He had evidently taken it out to check the time when he was killed. Now, to strike such a blow at a man whose head is bent forward requires a downward thrust at the relatively small target beneath the rear of the skull if one is to achieve the silent and instant death which you diagnose, Watson. It is more difficult.'

I cast my mind back to my brief examination of the dead man. 'When I lifted the man's head,' I recalled, 'the hilt of the knife protruded at a downward slant.'

'Well done, Watson, so it did. Now that indicates that, as the victim bent his head to look at his watch, he was struck in the neck by an almost horizontal thrust, and that, gentlemen, is a most uncommon way of wielding a short knife. To generate the maximum force, a stabber thrusts either upwards or downwards.'

He paused and Hopkins and I waited expectantly.

Fumbling in his pockets for his briar, he resumed.

'The curious angle of the blow made me wonder if it had, indeed, been a stabbing motion at all. A few feet to the rear of the bench is a clump of shrubbery. I examined that with care, finding what I expected – the marks in the soil of the shrubbery where a tall man with a lame left leg had stood and waited for some time.'

'I can see how you determined that he was lame, Mr Holmes, by the differing weight on his footprints, but what makes you say he was tall?' enquired Hopkins.

Holmes lit his pipe and, when it was drawing, smiled. 'Because, as he waited for his quarry, he bent down two small branches to improve his view of the bench. The height of his eyes was near enough that of mine, and I am a little over six feet tall.'

'But what about the blow with the knife?' I asked.

'I cannot prove it,' admitted Holmes, 'but I have a strong suspicion that the knife was thrown.'

'Thrown!' exclaimed the policeman. 'It would be an extremely accurate and a very forceful throw!'

'So it was,' agreed Holmes, 'but it accounts for the angle of the blow, and it led to my conclusion that the perpetrator was well-muscled. A weak man, however accurate his throw, could not have given the weapon sufficient force to drive it deeply into the neck.'

Hopkins nodded thoughtfully. 'And you're sure the knife is Scottish?' he said at last.

'At this point that might mean anything or nothing,' said Holmes. 'Those who claim Scottish blood and wear the ornamental dress with kilt and sporran typically wear a skean-dhu tucked into the top of a stocking, as their ancestors might have.'

'You're not suggesting,' said the police inspector, 'that the killer was wearing Highland costume?'

'No, Hopkins, I am not. I am merely pointing out that, although the weapon is uniquely Scottish, there are probably many of them to be found in London. You should also consider that it is a weapon designed for stabbing at close quarters and that someone who could throw it with such unerring accuracy must have had a great deal of practise with it. That, I submit, bespeaks a Scotsman.'

Hopkins nodded again. 'What did you make of the victim?' he asked.

'The American?' said Holmes.

'You think he was American?' said Hopkins. 'I grant you that his straw hat was bought in New York.'

'Well done,' said Holmes. 'Did you observe also that his cufflinks and his watch were American, and the cut of his boots suggested American manufacture?'

'I can't say that I did,' admitted the Scotland Yarder.

'No matter,' said Holmes. 'The watch may mean little. Most of the cheap pocket watches sold in Britain nowadays seem to be of American manufacture, but his was not a cheap one; it was a moderately expensive instrument by a decent firm of Massachusetts watchmakers, so it may well have been purchased there. Taken with the hat, the cufflinks and the cut of his boots, I believe we have an American or an Englishman who has lived there for some time. What do you make of the contents of his pockets?'

'There were virtually none,' said Hopkins. 'He carried no papers of any kind, nor any wallet nor pocketbook; there was no name or initials on his hat or clothing, and only one sovereign, six shillings and fourpence in loose change in his pocket. He wore no jewellery apart from the cufflinks, but a ring had been recently removed from the left hand. His watch, though a decent one, had no inscription or initials on it.'

'Excellent!' said Holmes. 'And what, pray, does that suggest?'

'That he was about some business which he thought might be dangerous and that he was anxious not to be recognized or identified – even to the extent of removing a ring from his hand.'

'Well done,' said my friend. 'I think I am right in saying that he carried no weapon of any kind?'

'None at all,' confirmed Hopkins.

'Then I would fault you on only one point, Hopkins. He did not, it seems, believe the business he was about to be dangerous. That he was anxious not to be identified is clear, but carrying a knife, a life preserver or even a firearm would not make him identifiable. No, Hopkins, he was not expecting trouble.'

'Then have you any theory as to what may have occurred, Mr Holmes?'

'We may collate a few observations,' said Holmes, and he began to strike his points off on the fingers of his left hand. 'Firstly, we have persons engaged in some variety of nefarious business (and let us assume for the present that there were two), who appoint a meeting in Regent's Park. Secondly, when Watson and I arrived, the victim was already dead and had been looking at his watch when he was killed. We came on the scene at a few minutes before two. It is not unreasonable to believe that their appointment was for two o'clock. Thirdly, he was killed before the time of his appointment.'

'Which means?' said the inspector.

'Which means one of two things, Hopkins. Either the person he intended to meet was more dangerous than he supposed, in which case they arrived early, hid themselves in the shrubbery and killed him when an opportunity presented, or a third party intervened.'

'In what way?' I asked.

'By coming to know of the meeting, arriving early and eliminating one of the parties to the appointment.'

'But we saw no one arrive at two,' I objected.

'True,' agreed Holmes, 'but I cannot avoid the overall facts – that the victim (who was quite intelligent enough to remove all traces of his identity) went openly to meet someone with no apparent hint of danger, yet he was skilfully and viciously killed at that rendezvous. I suspect that there is not only a missing murderer, there is also a missing second party who should have been there. That raises the question as to why that person was not at the rendezvous.'

Stanley Hopkins frowned. 'With the greatest respect, Mr Holmes, are we not becoming a bit theoretical?'

'Tush, Hopkins!' exclaimed Holmes. 'You are beginning to sound like dear old Lestrade or Toby Gregson. I have put before you reasonable inferences from what we know of the facts. There are many facts which we do not know – beginning with the murdered man's identity – but until we have more data I see nothing unreasonable in the propositions I have made.'

Hopkins was about to reply when Mrs Hudson arrived, accompanied by the uniformed sergeant we had seen in the park.

'I beg pardon for disturbing you, gentlemen, but there's an urgent message for Inspector Hopkins from the Yard,' said the sergeant.

'Then by all means deliver it, Sergeant,' said Holmes.

'It seems there's been a Scotch guest found murdered at the Braemar Hotel, sir. The superintendent wishes you to look into it, sir.'

'Thank you, Sergeant. Have you completed all the necessary work up in the park?'

'Yes, sir. The body has been removed to

the mortuary.'

'Do we have a cab, Sergeant?'

'I brought one to the door, sir.'

'Well done. Mr Holmes, I'm sorry to dash off like this, but needs must, as you see.'

'Not at all,' said Holmes. 'Would you have any objection if we were to accompany you, Inspector?'

'I'd be pleased, sir. Sergeant, catch hold of another cab so that Mr Holmes and the doctor can follow us.'

The sergeant touched his helmet and dashed away downstairs. Holmes and I collected our coats and sticks and followed Stanley Hopkins down to the street.

Once we were settled into a cab and following the inspector's vehicle I observed that Holmes' face bore, if not a smile, a certain expression of satisfaction.

'Holmes,' I said, 'why did you not tell Hopkins about the coded messages?'

'Because we know absolutely nothing about their meaning, Watson. How would they assist him?'

'Well,' I suggested, 'he might trace the persons who inserted them.'

'So he might,' said Holmes, 'and I shall try, but I'll wager you that all the messages were delivered to the newspaper's office by anonymous messenger boys bringing a text and the cash.'

'But you asked to accompany Hopkins to the Braemar in case the matter is connected with events in Regent's Park?'

'Of course,' he said. 'I do not say that murder by a Scotsman or murder of a Scotsman is extraordinary in a city the size of London, but for both to occur within a few hours on the same day, and at least one of them in connection with an affair which seems to have Jacobite connections, strikes me as interesting.'

Murder at the Braemar Hotel

It cannot be denied that there are places and landscapes which seem as though they were designed to be the setting of some gruesome crime. No one who has followed the track of the East End Murderer of the eighties through the foetid alleys of Whitechapel could doubt it. Yet Holmes has often pointed out to me that murder strikes in the country cottage as often as in the metropolitan slum, so it was no great surprise to me to discover that the Braemar Hotel was an institution which breathed respectability and in no way suggested violence or disorder.

It stood in a residential street in Kensington and its appearance made clear that two town houses had been adapted for commercial purposes. Those purposes were discreetly announced only by a brass plate on the left-hand pillar of the portico and the hotel's name with a thistle decoration wrought in coloured glass in the front door. A pale-faced maid opened the door to us and, when Hopkins had introduced himself, escorted us to a front parlour where Mrs McBride, the hotel's proprietress, awaited us.

The lady was small and silver-haired and, as she rose to greet us, it was evident to me that she was suffering from severe shock. Stanley Hopkins introduced us and succeeded in establishing that it was Mrs McBride herself who had discovered her guest's death when she called at his room. While the inspector, his sergeant and Holmes made their way upstairs, I took the lady's welfare into my hands and poured her a stiff measure of whisky from a decanter on the sideboard.

'You have suffered a severe shock, dear lady,' I said as I pressed the spirit upon her, 'which is entirely understandable, but Inspector Hopkins and Mr Holmes will wish to ask you a few questions once they have examined the scene of the incident. Now, I suggest that you take this stimulant, then have your maid prepare you a good strong cup of tea. After that you should feel better able to deal with affairs.'

I left her grasping the glass in two shaking hands, and made my way to the first floor, where the door of a front bedroom stood open. Holmes was not in sight, but Hopkins and his sergeant stood in the doorway. As I reached the landing, my friend appeared in the room's doorway and beckoned us in.

It was a large and pleasant room, with two windows opposite the door giving a view down on to the street. To the left of the windows stood a bed and there was a wardrobe behind the door and a washstand. Between the windows was a small writing table. The figure of a stocky man in early middle age was seated at the table, his head and shoulders slumped forward in a spreading pool of blood. I could see at once that he had been stabbed in precisely the same way as the Regent's Park victim, though the implement had not been left in the wound.

'The victim,' said Holmes, 'is, according to his pocketbook, a Mr Alistair McNair. He is – or was – a solicitor, or a Writer to the Signet, as they are styled in Scotland, practising at Perth. The railway ticket in his watch pocket reveals that he travelled to London four days ago. Unless I am wrong, Watson, I believe that he has been dead only a short time.'

I touched the dead man's clean-shaven cheek. 'I believe you are right,' I said. 'He seems to have been killed about lunchtime.'

'What do you believe has happened here, Mr Holmes?' asked Hopkins.

Holmes stood in the centre of the room and looked about him. 'McNair, from his dress, was evidently intending to go out. A person – we can reasonably infer a man – called on him. McNair knew that person and admitted him without question. They talked – for how long we do not know – then McNair turned to the table to write something. As he did so, his visitor seized the advantage and killed him with a blow to the neck. Taking the weapon and whatever McNair had written, the murderer then left the premises.'

'And the weapon?' queried Hopkins. 'Where did it come from and where has it gone?'

'Of that,' said Holmes, 'there can be no doubt. The weapon was obtained from there,' and he pointed to some items of clothing which had been laid out on the bed. I saw that they were the full dress costume worn by Highlanders at formal events.

My friend picked up from the bed a small black leather sheath, edged and tipped with silver and mounted with two slivers of decorative stone.

'There,' he said, showing the object to Hopkins, 'is the weapon's sheath. You have observed that the knife used in Regent's Park was ornamented by a so-called "Scotch pebble" – a piece of decorative agate in the butt. These two strips mounted here display the same striations as the stone set in the knife in the park. Having slain McNair with his own knife, the killer then took the weapon with him and used it on the American.'

He rummaged amongst the laid-out clothing, eventually producing a thick, oatmeal coloured stocking which clearly showed where a bloody knife had been wiped upon it.

'But what is this all about?' I asked.

'McNair,' said Holmes, 'travelled to London for a purpose we cannot, at present, determine. While here he inserted advertisements in the press, through which he made contact with the American.'

He reached around the dead lawyer and lifted a handful of newspaper cuttings from the writing table.

'You will find that these are the advertisements, and they will tell you nothing when you have deciphered them, apart from the fact that someone using the nom de plume "Charles Stuart" was making arrangements to meet someone who used the alias "Benjamin Franklin". That meeting was to have been in Regent's Park at two o'clock this afternoon. As I have already suggested, some third party came to know of the arrangement. He called here, extracted something in writing from McNair, then killed him and went off to the park to do the same to McNair's correspondent.'

Hopkins stared at the pieces of paper. 'You have deciphered these?' he said.

'Merely as an exercise in the first place,' said Holmes, 'but they revealed to me the place and time of the meeting, so I prevailed upon Watson to take a short stroll from our lodgings.'

Hopkins' fresh features lit up with a grin. 'I should have realized,' he said. 'You have always warned me to be suspicious of co-incidences. I should have realized that you were not in the park entirely by chance.'

He looked at the cuttings again. 'Benjamin Franklin! Charles Stuart!' he exclaimed. 'Have you no inkling as to the business they intended to transact, Mr Holmes?'

Holmes shook his head. 'The only connection I can make at present is that Franklin was an American Jacobite and that Charles Stuart was, of course, the so-called "Young Pretender" more familiarly known as "Bonnie Prince Charlie". Watson, however, scoffs at the connection.'

'Is this political, then?' asked Hopkins.

'I imagine that, if you lay this matter before your colleagues in the secret department, they will scoff louder than Watson. I suggest that you proceed on the basis that you have two unsolved murders committed by the same man and see where it leads.'

The Scotland Yarder nodded slowly. 'Then,' he said, 'I think we must find out what we can about Mr McNair. Let us have a word with Mrs McBride.'

We filed downstairs, leaving the sergeant to watch the room, and Mrs McBride's maid showed us back to the front parlour. The lady had evidently taken both my prescription and my advice, for she was seated behind a tea tray, looking a great deal more composed than before, though a small handkerchief was held in her left hand.

When we were all seated and had been offered and accepted tea, Inspector Hopkins leaned forward.

'I appreciate that this matter has been deeply distressing to you, Mrs McBride, but I'm sure you understand that it is my duty to ask you a few questions.'

The lady nodded. 'My husband and I kept this hotel for fourteen years, and I have carried it on for ten more since he passed over. I don't believe that either of us would ever imagine such a thing in our house. We tried to make it a homely place for Scots folk visiting London, and they seemed to appreciate it. Poor Mr McNair was a regular visitor and always said he appreciated our simple Scots food.'

'He visited regularly?' repeated Hopkins. 'About how often did he come and how long had he been doing so, Mrs McBride?'

'Oh, it'll be five years or thereabouts that he's been coming. Three or four times a year he would be in London on business.'

'Do you know what business brought him to London?' asked Holmes.

'Well, he was a Writer to the Signet – that's what we call a solicitor – and he was the man of business to one of the big lairds up in the Highlands. I think it was on the laird's business that he usually came to London, though I know that he liked London. He wasn't all business when he was here. He'd go to dinners and that. He was due to go out tonight, to a dinner at the London Scottish Society. I saw his clothes all laid out when I saw him in his room this morning.'

The recollection made her deploy her handkerchief, and Hopkins waited a moment before asking her, 'What time was that, Mrs McBride? As near as you recall.'

'It would have been about eleven,' she said. 'He rang the bell, and I was already upstairs, so I answered it. He told me that he had an appointment this afternoon and asked if I could let him have his luncheon early. He came down about noon and ate and went back to his room. He told me that he would be out from about half past one and that he wouldn't be in for dinner because of his evening engagement.'

42

'And what time did his visitor call?' enquired Holmes.

'That was just after he'd gone upstairs again, maybe about twenty before one. I heard Heather answer the front door and show somebody upstairs.'

'You never saw Mr McNair's visitor?' said Hopkins.

Mrs McBride shook her head. 'As I say, Heather let him in, and neither of us saw him leave. I don't know if Heather heard him go, but I didn't.'

She paused. 'It was a while later, maybe a quarter before two, when I minded that Mr McNair had said that he was going out for a two o'clock appointment. I hadn't heard him leave, and he was usually very good at calling out when he was going out, so I went up and tapped his door, just in case he was still with his visitor and had forgotten the time. There was no answer, so I looked in. That was when – when I found him.'

This time the memory renewed her distress and the tears flowed. We waited a while in silence, then Holmes said, 'You have done very well and helped us as much as you can. Perhaps we might have a word with your maid, Heather?'

The request brought Mrs McBride back to the present. Wiping her eyes she rang the bell and soon her maid was with us.

'Sit down, Heather,' commanded her employer. 'These gentlemen would like to ask you some questions about poor Mr McNair and his visitor. There is nothing to be afraid of.'

Heather sat primly on a straight-backed chair and folded her hands in her lap. She looked nervously from one to another of us.

Stanley Hopkins smiled at her encouragingly. 'Now then,' he began, 'you work here for Mrs McBride and your name is?'

'Heather, sir. Heather Mackenzie. I've been with Mrs McBride nearly two years.'

Hopkins nodded. 'And you answered the door at about twenty to one. Is that right?'

'Yes, sir. It was a caller for Mr McNair. Mr McNair had not long gone up to his room. I was going to show the visitor to the guests' parlour and call Mr McNair down, but the gentleman said he was an old friend of Mr McNair's from Scotland and asked me to take him to his room.'

'And was he a Scotsman?' asked Holmes.

'Oh, aye. Well, I think so, sir.'

'You're a Scot yourself, Heather. Did you recognize where his accent came from?'

'He was from the Highlands, sir. I've little doubt about that. I thought at first he was Irish, but he had that lilt that you only hear in the Highlands.'

'Very good,' said Holmes. 'Now, can you

tell us what you remember of this gentleman? What he looked like? How he was dressed?'

My friend, who could be dramatically abrasive when he wished, had an almost hypnotic ability to calm nervous women or children. It had worked on Heather Mackenzie and now she was entirely anxious to assist.

'It's a bit difficult, sir,' she said. 'I was in the dining room, serving the guests luncheon when the bell rang. I ran through to the front door—' She paused. 'He was a big man, I think. Maybe as tall as you, sir, because I remember I saw his shadow on the glass as I went down the hall.'

She paused again. 'When I opened the door he was on the top step. He lifted his hat and said, "Is this where my old friend Alistair McNair bides?" I told him Mr McNair was here and offered to take him to the guests' parlour, but he said, "Don't put him to the trouble. Just show me his room and I'll knock." Well, sir, I was taken up with serving the luncheon, so I was glad he didn't want me to bring Mr McNair down, so I took him to the foot of the stair and I pointed out the right door. I saw him go up and as I was turning away I heard Mr McNair opening the door to him.'

'And what did Mr McNair say? Did he

45

sound cheerful, or angry?' asked Holmes.

Heather shook her head. 'No, sir. He sounded more surprised than anything. All I heard him say was, "What are you doing in London?", then I was away to the dining room.'

'And you did not hear the visitor leave?' asked Hopkins.

'Oh, no, sir. I would have been between the kitchen and the dining room and I wouldn't hear the front door if it was shut quietly. He might have walked quietly down and gone out with nobody the wiser.'

Holmes nodded. 'Now,' he said, 'you have told us that the visitor was a man as tall as I am, who spoke like a Highlander. Is there anything more you can tell us about him? How was he dressed, for example?'

The girl looked up and concentrated, then she said, 'He was wearing a long duster coat and a hat much like yours, sir. Oh, and he had a stick, a heavy ash stick with a horn handle. He limped a bit as he went upstairs.'

'And you cannot tell us anything about his face?' asked my friend.

She shook her head. 'No, sir. I'm afraid I didnae mind him that much. I was taken up with serving luncheon. No, I cannae recall his features at all.'

'Never mind,' said Holmes. 'You have done very well.' Turning aside, Holmes asked of the landlady, 'Tell me, Mrs McBride, are the rooms on either side of Mr McNair's occupied?'

'No,' she said. 'The left-hand room is unoccupied at present and the right-hand one is let to a Mrs Forwell, who is in Brighton visiting relatives this week.'

Holmes stood up. 'You have both been very helpful,' he said. 'Now you will want to put the whole unpleasant business behind you. Inspector Hopkins' men will see to the removal of Mr McNair and his effects.'

He turned to the door and the inspector and I rose to follow, but Holmes turned back.

'Just one more thing,' he said. 'Do you, by any chance, recall the name of the landowner for whom Mr McNair worked?'

Mrs McBride looked thoughtful. 'I know it, I'm sure I do. It's on the tip of my tongue. It's a queer name for a Scottish laird, it sounds partly foreign...'

'Was it,' asked Holmes, 'Czernowski-Stuart?'

'Aye! That's it! I said it sounded awfully queer for a Scotsman.'

A Plea from America

As we left the Braemar Hotel, Hopkins consulted Holmes. 'Have you any real idea what this is all about, Mr Holmes?' he asked.

Holmes shook his head. 'No real idea,' he said, 'but a number of unformed hypotheses. Despite today's events there is still a lack of data.'

'But where will you seek it?' asked the Scotland Yarder.

'Despite the two killings having occurred in London, it is evident that the affair has a Scottish element. I suspect that more data might be found by talking to McNair's client, the Laird of Strathcullar.'

'Is that the man you asked Mrs McBride about?'

'It is,' confirmed Holmes. 'His name is Czernowski-Stuart and he may be found, so far as I know, at his Castle of Strathcullar in the Highlands.'

He bade Hopkins good day and we stepped into our cab.

As we travelled back to Baker Street I turned recent events over in my mind, but ended as confused as when I began.

'Holmes,' I said at last, 'how did you come to know the name of this obscure Scottish laird?'

'This "obscure Scottish laird" as you call him, Watson, is the present holder of a title which is well-known in the Highlands and elsewhere. When I first established my practice in Montague Street, paying clients were infrequent and I had a good deal of time to pursue my researches into ancient charters at the British Museum. It was in the reading room there that I made the acquaintance of two brothers, Scots, who were indefatigable enquirers into Scottish lore and the history of the clans. They are both dead, but the present Laird of Strathcullar is some kind of relative of theirs.'

'I don't,' I said, 'see how that led you to deduce that he was McNairn's client.'

'Forgive me,' he said. 'My question of Mrs McBride was not asked on the basis of a pure guess. You know how I despise guesswork. It arose because, as I have already explained to you, this matter seems to have a Jacobite dimension. The brothers Czernowski-Stuart always claimed that they were the heirs of Bonnie Prince Charlie and that, thereby, the elder one was the true King of England and Scotland. I not unreasonably inferred that the present laird will spring from the same line and have the same claim.'

I stared at him in amazement.

'Then you still believe that this affair is all about a new Jacobite plot?' I said.

He smiled. 'Watson! We had this conversation some hours ago. I do not fear a ravening horde of kilted Celts swarming over our northern border. The Czernowski-Stuarts, so far as I know, have never pressed their claim to the throne and I cannot imagine them doing so violently. Nevertheless, the confirmation that one of the murdered men was the man of business of the Laird of Strathcullar supports my contention that it all has something to do with the cause of the white rose.'

'So that is why you advised Hopkins to pursue his enquiries in Scotland,' I said.

'Precisely, Watson. Whether the good inspector will take my advice I know not, but you and I shall certainly go to the Highlands, probably tomorrow if it will not inconvenience you.'

'Not at all, Holmes,' I said, looking forward to a summer sojourn in the Highlands.

Holmes spent the remainder of the day in consulting maps of Scotland, checking train departures in Bradshaw's and firing off reply-paid telegrams and consulting with our Scots landlady. It was when she served our supper that Mrs Hudson brought also a reply to one of my friend's wires, the reading of which evidently pleased him.

'Our arrangements are complete, Watson,' he announced. 'We have accommodation in Strathcullar itself. If we leave London about midday we shall be there early the following morning.'

As it fell out, our plans were altered by a postcard which lay beside my plate when I came down to breakfast next morning. It bore the emboss of the American Bookshop in Charing Cross Road and a short message:

Dear Dr Watson,
The volume you requested is to hand.
Perhaps you will call and collect it.

Both Holmes and I knew that it meant more than it said, for though the American Bookshop did deal in books, it was also the post from which one of America's presidential aides – an extremely senior intelligence agent – observed events in Britain. We had been introduced to the situation by Mycroft Holmes at the time of the old Queen's Jubilee and the plot against her by an insane American.*

*See my *Sherlock Holmes and the Royal Flush*

I passed the card to Holmes.

'I have ordered no book,' I said. 'Evidently the United States believes it has business with you.'

'Indeed,' he agreed, 'and since the Scottish affair appears to involve America in some way, it seems reasonable to delay our departure a little and see what our transatlantic friends require.'

So it was that later the same morning we visited the shop and I presented the postcard to a young assistant in horn-rimmed spectacles, who promptly disappeared into the rear of the premises, but was back in a moment with a request that we wait upon the manager in his upstairs office.

When our guide introduced us to the shop's manager, both Holmes and I were surprised to note that it was not the man with whom we had dealt previously.

'A new incumbent,' remarked Holmes as we both shook hands with a tall, greying man with a moustache who gave his name as Colonel Beaumont Swice.

'My predecessor has completed his time in London. Our service rotates us so that the natives will not become too familiar with us or us with them. For some reason my superiors regard London as a dangerous posting insomuch as more than one of my predecessors has decided to retire here.'

We laughed and seated ourselves on two chairs in front of his desk.

'Now, Colonel,' said Holmes, once we were seated, 'I imagine that the duties of a presidential aide remain as before – to watch these islands with a view to detecting matters of interest to the United States which are of no interest to Britain or in which you would not expect British assistance.'

'That's correct,' said Swice. 'In addition, if events are taking place here which are detrimental to my country's interests, I attempt to intervene, always in the knowledge that I must in no way embarrass my own government or His Majesty's.'

Holmes gave a satisfied nod. 'You will have been told that Watson and I have assisted this office before and maintained the confidentiality of that matter. So long as your affairs do not in any way threaten the Empire's wellbeing, then I am prepared to place my talents at your disposal again.'

'Thank you, Mr Holmes,' said the colonel, and straightened the papers on his desk before looking up. 'You need have no fear that the present matter will cause you such a problem. Indeed, my superiors had considered placing the affair in the hands of Scotland Yard, but were too embarrassed.'

'Embarrassed!' repeated Holmes. A thin

smile appeared. 'It seems to me that little embarrasses your nation, Colonel. It must be a singular affair indeed.'

'It is,' said Swice, 'and one that might also embarrass Great Britain and France. It is not, however, embarrassment that concerns my superiors, it is the safety and security of our country.'

It was evident that the colonel was entirely serious. Holmes leaned back in his seat and began to rub the thumb of his left hand, always a sign of anticipation.

'I do not know how much you gentlemen know about the foundation of the United States,' began Swice, 'nor about the attempts there have been to overthrow it...'

'We are aware,' said Holmes, 'that a singularly stupid English government imposed trading restrictions and taxes upon the American colonies which so enraged them that the War of Independence resulted, which, by equally enormous mismanagement, we contrived to lose. We are also aware of the fact that Aaron Burr raised a rebellion against the fledgling republic less than a century ago and that the desire of the Confederacy to leave the Union led to a bitter and bloody conflict.'

Swice nodded. 'Nor can you be unaware,' he said, 'that we have recently lost our president at the hands of an assassin.'

'Surely,' I said, 'the president was slain by an insane anarchist acting alone? Czolgosz's deed was that of a madman, not a revolutionary!'

'It suits my country to let the world believe so,' replied Swice, 'but the death of President McKinley was one of a series of acts intended to create disunity and confusion in the Union. You have referred to the war between the states as "bitter", Mr Holmes, but I doubt if you have any real idea of the depth to which that bitterness runs in some southerners.'

'Are you suggesting that the Confederacy might rise again?' I asked. 'Surely there will always be those who dream of an independent south, but they cannot seriously believe it to be a possibility?'

Swice sighed wearily. 'I wish that were so, Doctor. In fact it is a possibility and events are in motion which make that possibility more realistic.'

He paused. 'When the United States was founded there was not, initially, a unanimous view that she should become a republic. While all were agreed that the colonies must free themselves from the rule of King George, there were those who believed that the only proper way to do so was by acquiring another monarch – one more to their liking.'

He paused once more, but Holmes and I were silent. To me, at any rate, this was a revelation.

'It is fairly widely known that the Continental Congress offered George Washington what amounted to the crown of the United States on at least two, maybe three, occasions. He was wise enough to refuse each time. What is far less known is that a delegation approached Charles James Stuart, the Jacobite claimant to the throne of England and Scotland, and invited him to accept the monarchy of America.

'He refused, apparently on the basis that he had no heir and that, were he to accept, on his death England might try to seize her old colonies again.'

'I confess that is news to me,' said Holmes, and I agreed.

'He did, however, do the emergent United States a favour – or tried. He negotiated a loan from the French of one hundred thousand gold angels, to assist the colonists in their rebellion. It could be seen as a self-less gesture, but the French were interested in anything that would cause difficulties for Britain and Charles Stuart had his own motive. He had his own currency minted while in exile – a gold angel with his own head on it. It was not the most widely valued or accepted currency in Europe, so that the opportunity to sell a large quantity to the French was welcome to him. From the French point of view, if the British discovered the transaction they would probably believe that it was Charles Stuart who was meddling in their affairs.'

'This is all very interesting,' remarked Holmes, 'but you have yet to explain how that matter concerns you today and why you require my assistance.'

Colonel Swice raised a hand to enjoin patience.

'The gold was shipped from the Netherlands to Scotland. The plan was to transport it across Scotland in the care of loyal Jacobite sympathizers, thereby evading Royal Navy patrols around the south and north of Britain. Once it reached a small port in the west of Scotland, a neutral ship would take it on board and risk crossing the Atlantic with it.'

He drew a deep breath before continuing. 'The plan,' he said, 'went wrong, insofar as King George's spies came to hear of it while the gold was still in Scotland. A huge force of redcoats was sent post-haste to the Highlands, to comb the country for the gold and interrogate any Jacobite who might know of it. They harried the country for months, but they found nothing.'

'The gold got to America?' I said.

'No, Doctor. The gold stayed hidden in Scotland, where, so far as anyone knows, it still remains.'

'Colonel Swice,' said Holmes, 'I hope you are not about to ask me to undertake a search for that gold. Surely the United States does not need it now?'

The colonel shook his head. 'No, Mr Holmes. Uncle Sam can manage well enough without that gold, but we don't want our enemies to lay their hands on it.'

'Your enemies?' I queried.

'The madmen who killed President Mc-Kinley,' he replied. 'If they were to lay their hands on those angels they would form a mighty contribution to their war chest and allow them to unleash all manner of harm in the States.'

'Is there any serious likelihood of that happening?' asked Holmes. 'The gold has been lost for more than a century. Half the British Army failed to find it. For all we know it may have been found and disbursed on good whisky.'

'I think not, Mr Holmes. The Charles Stuart gold angel is an unusual coin and not many turn up in Scotland. I have had coin dealers and money changers all over Britain on the lookout for them for some time. Nevertheless, until days ago I might have agreed with you,' said the American, 'but events have taken an ominous turn and it appears that someone may know where Bonnie Prince Charlie's angels are hidden.'

'Now that,' said Holmes, 'is a great deal more interesting,' and he fell to rubbing his thumb again. 'What makes you think so?'

'One of the operatives employed in the States to track the conspirators who murdered the president, a certain Captain Carter, intercepted a message which revealed that some of the conspirators intended to travel to Scotland, with a view to laying their hands on what their message called "the French gold that went missing in Scotland at the time of the Revolution". Captain Carter's information set alarm bells ringing in Washington, where a search of records dating back to the War of Independence confirmed that there had indeed been such a gift from the French which had vanished in Scotland. Captain Carter was ordered to pursue the plotters to Britain and report to me.'

He paused once more and his long face grew even more solemn.

'Carter arrived and informed me that he was on his way to Scotland on the heels of his quarry. Subsequently he came back to London and reported that he had found someone who he believed had access to the gold or knowledge of its whereabouts and that he was making arrangements to meet them.'

'And he went to meet that person in Regent's Park yesterday,' said Holmes, 'where he was ambushed and murdered, as was the informant he intended to meet.'

'Indeed,' agreed Swice.

There was a short silence, then, 'Have you informed Scotland Yard of Captain Carter's identity?' asked Holmes.

'I have,' said Swice. 'I have told them that he was an acquaintance of mine from our days in the army, that he came to Britain on some business unknown to me, and that he visited me twice while he was here.'

Holmes nodded. 'So you have given them no indication of Carter's business in this country, nor of your specific connection with him?'

'No,' agreed Swice. 'I told you earlier that at one point Washington considered placing the whole matter in the hands of Scotland Yard or of one of your military intelligence agencies, but there are too many embarrassing aspects to it. Apart from the question of the source of the gold and the purposes for which it was provided, if the gold is found, the question will arise as to whom it belongs – the United States? The French? The British Crown?'

'I can see that it might provide some ticklish diplomatic questions,' said Holmes. 'Nevertheless, you wish me to find it – if it can be found?'

'The United States cannot risk such a sum falling into the hands of the conspirators. By the murder of Mr McKinley they have proved their ruthlessness and their organizational ability. If they have funds as well, they will be able to buy influence, to advertise their cause, to corrupt officials, to buy arms – who knows where it will end.'

Holmes nodded again, then stood.

'Unless,' he said, 'there is anything more that you can tell me, Colonel, I think it is time that Watson and I were on our way to Scotland.'

Holmes Pursues a Theory

Our interview with Colonel Swice had radically altered our travelling plans and it was evening before we were able to take a train from King's Cross. We knew it would be neither a short nor a simple journey. Holmes' research had shown that Strathcullar lay well beyond any railway line; while the main line would take us as far as Inverness, we would then need to take a local train for some distance, followed by a road journey to our ultimate destination.

We had made ourselves comfortable in our compartment and the train was steaming out of King's Cross, when I decided to take the opportunity to question Holmes about the whole affair.

'What is it that you do not understand, Watson?' he asked, with a touch of impatience. 'The facts – so far – are simple and the realistic conclusions that may be drawn are fairly evident.'

'I was confused enough yesterday,' I said, 'when you deciphered those advertisements and began to talk about Jacobites. Now we have two murders in London – one of them an American spy; a connection to the murder of Mr McKinley; and a missing hoard of gold, though I grant your prediction of a Jacobite connection seems to have some substance.'

He nodded his head with a satirical smile. 'The facts we have at present are eminently simple,' he said, and leaning forward began to strike off points on his long fingers.

'Firstly, I observed that two persons were in covert communication through a newspaper. Decipherment of their messages revealed a suggestion of a Jacobite connection, an American connection and a planned meeting by the Clarence Gate.'

It was my turn to nod, without any sarcasm.

'Secondly,' he continued, 'an American attended that meeting and was murdered. We now know him to have been Captain Carter of the United States Treasury's secret service and we know the reasons why he was in England.

'Thirdly,' he went on, 'a Scottish lawyer was murdered at the Braemar Hotel. He appears to have been the other party to the newspaper advertisements.

'Fourthly,' he concluded, 'Colonel Swice has now revealed to us a background which should be sufficient for you to make reasonable inferences as to what is going forward.'

I shook my head slowly. 'You appear,' I said, 'to be saying that Colonel Swice's information puts the whole thing in perspective, but I admit that I was confused yesterday and I am even more so today.'

'Watson,' he chided, 'the colonel has requested my assistance precisely because he does not have all the pieces of the puzzle, but what he does know permits a line of inference which may resolve the matter or at least bring in further data.'

'Then what inference do you draw?' I asked. 'Have you a theory?'

'I have warned you often, Watson, that it is an error of the greatest magnitude to theorize too far ahead of the available data, but it is permissible, and often necessary, to take the known data and see what chains of logic may be extended therefrom. It may be a very useful exercise, so long as one's postulations are realistic and do not extend too far ahead of the known facts.'

He took out his cigarette case and we both lit cigarettes.

'Let us assume,' he said, 'that we are right in believing that the cryptic advertisements were messages between McNair and Carter. I think you will agree that there is little doubt there.'

I nodded and he went on.

'Since both parties evidently knew the topic which they needed to discuss, there was no reason to refer to it in the messages. They were simply used to arrange a meeting.'

'But we know that Carter was looking for the French gold!' I said.

'Precisely, Watson! You see, a little encouragement sets your brain working. Since we now know Carter's object, it is reasonable to assume that McNair was in the process of offering Carter something which he wanted.'

'You mean that McNair was offering the gold – or knowledge of its whereabouts!' I exclaimed.

'Exactly so, Watson.'

An objection occurred to me. 'But, if McNair was dishonest – and it seems he was – he would surely have made away with the gold himself?'

'There are numerous possible reasons why he might not have done,' said Holmes, 'not the least of which is the rarity of Prince Charlie's angels. The sudden emergence of quantities of such a coin would undoubtedly have raised enquiries. How much better to sell them at discount to Carter, who would have means to dispose of them without attracting undue attention.'

I nodded again, though I was not entirely convinced.

'So,' I said, 'McNair and Carter have made an appointment in the park, but both of them are murdered. Who killed them? It seems to have been the work of the same man.'

Holmes drew on his cigarette. 'There,' he said, 'we must be careful that we do not allow our theory to extend too far. What I have suggested so far is reasonable and realistic and does not conflict with anything we know. To go on to attempt to identify the killer without further data would be pure speculation.'

'How so?' I asked.

'Because, Watson, all we know of the man is his physical description – which he may have changed – and the virtually certain fact that he is a Scot or can pass as such. Motive would be of great assistance, but we do not know what that was.'

'Surely it was to acquire the gold?' I said. 'And although he was a Scot, is it not conceivable that he was acting on behalf of the American conspiracy in trying to acquire the gold?'

'Certainly,' agreed my friend, 'but there, Watson, you fall headlong into the very danger against which I so recently warned you. He may be a Scottish agent of the

American conspiracy; he may be someone who already knows the whereabouts of the gold and seeks to protect it; he may be someone who sought, as you suggest, to obtain whatever information McNair may have had; he may be a loyal Jacobite who seeks to preserve the gold for Scotland's purposes; or he may be a plain and simple thief. He might even be a French agent, seeking to recover their unused gift.'

'But those are all pure speculations!' I protested.

'So, Watson, is your own theory. We simply do not have sufficient data to theorize further without the risk of serious error. That is why we are travelling to Scotland – to acquire further data if it can be found.'

He leaned back in his seat and picked up a newspaper. Snapping it open he disappeared behind it and I realized that our discussion was at an end.

By dinnertime Holmes had read all the newspapers he had brought and was good company in the dining car, where his conversation covered an enormous number of topics, each one of which he treated with the authority of someone who had carried out a special study of the subject, rather than that of a casual reader. Nevertheless, he did not once refer to our current enquiry, and I realized that he had meant what he said earlier on – that he had explored the case in his mind so far as the established facts permitted; that he had drawn certain inferences from those facts; and that he had now put the matter entirely out of his mind until he could obtain new information.

It was early morning when a change of engines at Carlisle permitted us to take advantage of the station's coffee room for a few minutes. While we drank our coffee a familiar voice hailed us and Inspector Hopkins appeared beside our table.

'We did not know you were on the train,' said Holmes, when Hopkins was seated.

'Ah, well, Mr Holmes, Scotland Yard does not, I'm sorry to say, permit officers of the rank of inspector and below to travel by first class.'

'Then, since we cannot promote you, Hopkins, you must allow me to make up your ticket so that you may share our compartment.'

Hopkins shook his head. 'It's very kind of you to offer, Mr Holmes, but that would be taken by my superiors as my receiving a favour of value from a member of the public.'

My friend shook his head in wonderment. 'Where are you bound for, anyway, Hopkins?'

'Inverness,' he replied. 'I have to look into the late Mr McNair's practice and talk to partners and family and so on. What brings you and the doctor to Scotland, Mr Holmes?'

'I might tell you that Watson must revisit the land of his forebears, or that we are motivated by his belief in the rejuvenating effects of a rural atmosphere, but in reality we are bound to Strathcullar to pursue the apparent Jacobite connections of the Regent's Park killing and the murder of McNair.'

Hopkins frowned. 'Do you seriously believe that there is a Jacobite element in the case, Mr Holmes?'

'Oh, certainly,' said Holmes. 'But it is not one that should bother the secret department at the Yard. Nevertheless, I advise you to bear it always in mind.'

We re-boarded our train and I congratulated Holmes on his kind offer to Hopkins.

'Nonsense!' he said. 'There is nothing I wished for less than to pass the time between here and Inverness fending off Hopkins' questions about the case, for I could not tell him a quarter of what I told you earlier. I rather thought that Metropolitan Police rules would prevent him accepting my offer.'

I could not but smile at his tactic and

observe that he was being scrupulously careful to obey our client's instruction and to tell Scotland Yard nothing that would embarrass America.

On the platform at Inverness we took a farewell of Hopkins, who went off about his business in that city. It was also there that I noticed two men waiting for the local train who, by the cut of their clothing and their accents, were Americans.

When the little stopping train had arrived and we had taken a compartment, I remarked to Holmes on the presence of the two Americans.

'I observed them,' he said. 'Did you note their luggage?'

'They had a number of bags, but I noticed nothing in particular. To what do you wish to draw my attention?'

'The absence of guns or fishing rods,' he replied. 'Still, it may be that they are innocent walkers, as are we, eh, Watson?'

Our train wound interminably through hills and valleys, stopping frequently at remote stations and halts where no one seemed to board or leave the train. The Americans remained with it until we reached our destination. When we emerged from the little station there were two carriages drawn up outside, one that Holmes had booked by telegram and another which took the Americans. Their driver took them away at a smart pace, but ours was of a more reflective character so we were soon left behind. Nevertheless, we were able to see that they had departed in the direction of Strathcullar.

Our road took us through some beautiful and dramatic country, but our journey from London had been a long one and the upholstery and springs of our equipage left a deal to be desired. I was soon wishing that we were seated in our lodgings with a good Scots meal set before us.

At length, Holmes, who had studied the map of the area, said to our jarvey, 'We cannot now be far from Strathcullar, can we?'

We were pulling slowly up a long steep pass, and our driver made no immediate reply. However, as we reached the top he reined in beside a tall pillar of dark granite and pointed with his whip.

'There's your destination, gentlemen. It'll be only minutes the noo.'

Below us lay a broad valley framed between two ranges of lofty hills, on the tops of which there were still lingering smears of snow. Most of the valley was filled with a great lake, or more properly loch, which narrowed slightly towards its further end. The shores were dotted with small islands and two larger islands lay well out into the water. The furthest and lesser one had a small building of some kind upon it and stone walls, but its larger neighbour carried a handsome square building, decorated at each corner by the conical turrets which are so characteristic of Scotland.

'What,' I asked, 'is the flag that flies from the large building on the island?'

'That,' said our driver, 'is Strathcullar Castle, the laird's home, and that flag is the Stuart flag, the banner of the good old cause.'

I was a little disconcerted to find this flaunted openly in Britain and turned my attention to the lakeside, where a row of houses and a jetty faced across to the castle. I had to admit that the afternoon sun lighting the rippling loch like shimmering silver made a brave view of our new location.

The driver whipped up his horse and we trundled downwards into Strathcullar.

A Reconnaissance

Soon we drew up outside a white cottage on the loch's foreshore, part of a long row which seemed to form Strathcullar's only street.

A pleasant-faced woman stepped out of the door to meet us. 'You'll be Kirsty Hudson's two gentlemen,' she said. 'You're very welcome.' To our driver she issued a command, 'Wullie, take the gentlemen's bags up tae their room. Ye ken whaur it is. While you do that I'll be aboot mashing a drop of tea.'

I had heard nothing so welcome for hours and was very glad to seat myself at a table spread with a snow-white cloth, on which lay a plate of oatcakes, a dish of butter and a jar of strawberry conserve.

'Have a drop of tea noo,' suggested our landlady, as she poured the tea, 'then make yourselves at hame upstairs and when you're settled I'll do you a proper Scots meal.'

Mrs Mackintosh, for that was her name, was as good as her word. Holmes and I took possession of a large and comfortable bed-room upstairs with a view across the fore-shore and the jetty of the castle and much of the loch. After disposing of our luggage we returned downstairs to find our landlady busy preparing dinner and when it was served it met fully her advance notice. So it was that, tired by our travels and replete from Mrs Mackintosh's cooking, I sprawled opposite Holmes across the parlour fire while we smoked a last pipe each.

'She is as good a cook as Mrs Hudson,' I remarked to Holmes.

He chuckled. 'Never dare to tell Mrs Hudson so or we shall be looking for new diggings!'

'I must admit,' I said, 'that I wonder why anyone would want to make their home in London when there are places like this.'

Holmes eyed me fishily. 'It must,' he said, 'be your rural childhood that makes you slip so readily into the bucolic mode. Never-theless, you should at all times remember that this is not a holiday excursion. We are carrying out a mission of grave importance to the United States and seeking a ruthless and skilful killer. Do not drop your guard because the scenery is beautiful and the people soft-spoken, Watson.'

'You consider this a dangerous matter?' I asked.

'You saw the bodies of Carter and McNair and you know that both were killed in cold blood. With a killer of that ilk in the picture and a hoard of gold at stake, I would suggest that we are in very dangerous waters indeed.'

He drew on his pipe, then knocked it out on the fire grate. 'With that in mind,' he added, 'I think we should make a reconnaissance tomorrow.'

The next morning Holmes woke me early and, taking a package of food prepared by Mrs Mackintosh, we set out. It was Sunday, but we excused ourselves from worship in the village kirk, Holmes telling our hostess that we were inveterate walkers whose real worship of the Creator was in the open air.

Holmes set a brisk pace along the foreshore road, making towards the pass by which we had arrived in Strathcullar. The sun was fairly well above the far end of the loch when we reached the granite pillar where we had halted on the previous day.

My friend dropped his knapsack at the foot of the pillar, extracted his binoculars from it and seated himself on a nearby boulder, from which he began a careful scan of the valley. I confess that I began a grateful examination of Mrs Mackintosh's cold meat sandwiches.

Beneath us a bell began to chime from the kirk in the village and, when I looked, I saw that a boat was setting out from the castle. Holmes turned his glasses on it for a moment or two, then passed them to me.

I saw that the boat contained three people: a tall man who sat in the stern, a slighter man, more formally dressed, and a stocky youth at the oars. At the boat's stern a staff displayed the same flag that flew over Strathcullar Castle.

'The laird is evidently fulfilling his religious duties,' remarked Holmes, 'and that fearsome individual at the stern will be his manservant.' And he took the glasses back.

I had finished my refreshments and was sprawled on the grass and heather, almost dozing I admit, when something struck the granite pillar and two shots rang out from the hillside above the pass.

In my years of military service and in the decades since I believe that I have never met a man as cool under fire as Sherlock Holmes. As the shots still echoed in the hillsides he grabbed my arm and dragged me behind the tall stone, rolling rapidly after me. Once we were out of the line of fire he took the binoculars and began cautiously to peer around either side of our stronghold.

'He is – or was – up by the waterfall, in the bracken,' he remarked after a few moments, and passed me the glasses. I took them and scanned the northern hillside, where a waterfall broke and tumbled almost parallel to the road downhill to enter the eastern end of the loch. The area was certainly well-covered with young bracken and would make an excellent hiding place, but I saw no sign of our assailant.

'I cannot see him,' I said.

'Nor did I,' replied Holmes, 'but if you look a little below the first fall of the water, on this side of the stream, you will see that some of the bracken is freshly broken.'

I looked again and saw that he was right.

'Are you sure it was not a careless huntsman?' I ventured. 'This is shooting country.'

'One,' said Holmes, 'the season is too early; two, the shots were from a pistol, not a rifle; three, the shooter knew his target. If you look at the front of this stone in due course, you will see that both bullets struck inches above my head. Had I not turned to replace my glasses in the knapsack they would have taken me. Now, if you have left any of Mrs Mackintosh's sandwiches, Watson, perhaps you will be good enough to pass me one.'

Munching a sandwich from one hand and with his other holding the field glasses, he lay for some time, minutely scanning the area about the waterfall.

After a while I asked a question that had occurred to me. 'How did he know our business and where to find us?'

'A good question, Watson. I suspect that we have been recognized by a combination of village gossip about Mrs Mackintosh's new lodgers and those illustrated romances about me which you create. To anyone connected with the London murders it would be no great leap of deduction to connect our appearance in Strathcullar with the affair. As to how he ambushed us – we told no one where we were going. Nobody could have known until we left Mrs Mackintosh's and set out in this direction, and I am certain no one followed us directly. I infer that someone watched our lodgings this morning from across the loch, or from one of the islands. Most probably from the far side of the loch. When they saw the direction of our travel, they skirted the northern shore of the lake and followed the course of the stream up to the waterfall.'

'Clever,' I said.

'As you have just pointed out, Watson, this is hunting country. The people make their living by tracking wild animals. We would have been easy.'

'What shall we do now?' I asked.

'Do?' he echoed. 'Why, nothing. Once I have completed my luncheon, we might take a trip to the waterfall and see what evidence our would-be killer has left behind.'

'Should we not go after him now?' I asked. 'I have my pistol.'

He chuckled amiably. 'Good old Watson! Always ready for the game. No, I think we had best give him plenty of time to withdraw before we move. To assault that steep slope, where every frond of bracken will signal our movements, in the face of such marksmanship as his, would be extremely foolish.'

So we remained, and Holmes kept his glasses on the waterfall. It was some long time before he gave a quietly satisfied cry.

'Aah!' he exclaimed. 'He is going.'

'How can you tell?' I asked.

'Because he has slid through the bracken below the waterfall and is moving downstream. The bracken gives his movement away.'

We waited another long while, until my friend was sure that the gunman was well down the hillside, then we cautiously emerged from our stronghold.

Holmes showed me where two bullets had struck splinters from the face of the ancient pillar. 'If nothing else,' he said, 'this little episode underlines the warning I gave you last night and serves as a reminder to me to take my own advice. In future we must go very cautiously indeed.'

We clambered up to the waterfall, and there it was possible to confirm that Holmes had been right. Even I could readily see that someone had emerged from the bracken on the far side of the stream, waded the stream and settled into a hiding place in the bracken where he would have had a good view of our position by the pillar.

Sherlock Holmes was soon upon hands and knees, magnifying glass in hand, poring over the area where our would-be assassin had hidden.

'Aha!' he exclaimed suddenly, showing me a palm scattered with small brown fragments. 'He rolled a cigarette here. He was careful enough not to leave the end, but he ignored the spillage as he rolled it.'

He sniffed at the threads of tobacco. 'Virginian,' he said, 'which makes it virtually certain that our attacker is American.'

'American!' I said. 'But I thought you believed that the murderer of McNair and Carter was a Scotsman?'

'So I do,' he said. 'This is a different man. Look at his length and build, where he has lain in the bracken. He is stockier than our Regent's Park killer. See his footprints by the stream. He walks differently and he does not limp.'

'Then we are up against two assassins!' I exclaimed.

'At least, Watson. Come, let us make our way home. Today has been very useful.'

We dropped down the hillside to the old pillar and made for the village, Holmes setting a cracking pace. He seemed to be in high good humour and hummed to himself as he strode along.

As we sat to dinner in our lodgings my friend questioned Mrs Mackintosh about Americans in the village.

'Och aye,' she said. 'We see more and more of them nowadays. They come for the hunting and the fishing or, like yourselves, for the walking. Mrs Drummond has two staying the noo, arrived the same day as yourselves.'

'I believe we saw them on the train,' said Holmes, 'but they did not seem to have any sporting luggage.'

She shook her head. 'They're walkers too,' she said. 'They'll disappoint Red Ewan and his pal.'

'Who are they?' asked Holmes.

'Red Ewan – his real name is Ewan Fergus Breck – is the laird's man, his servant, but he hasnae all that many duties, so he makes a wee bit from the hunters by ghillying for them. His great pal is Tam Chater. He's an

American himself, but he lives here in the village. He knows the hills pretty near as well as Red Ewan and goes ghillying as well.'

'Really?' said Holmes. 'It is an unusual place to find a native of the United States.'

'Aye,' she agreed. 'Ewan Breck left here as a young man. Like many more he went to America and he was gone for years. When he came back he'd been in Alaska gold mining and heaven knows what and Tam came with him. He's lived here ever since.'

'Well, Watson,' said Holmes, when we had retired to our bedchamber, 'today has been more successful than I expected.'

'If you mean,' I said, 'that you have not been murdered by an unknown lunatic in the hills—'

'Oh, quite so,' he interrupted me, 'but we learned a great deal from that episode.'

'If you mean that we learned to keep our pistols handy and to keep a sharp eye about us—'

'Of course,' he interrupted me again. 'But more to the point we have learned that somebody – most probably an American – fears our involvement in affairs at Strathcullar and that there are at present no less than three Americans in the village and one native who has lived in America.' He rubbed his hands gleefully. 'I admit, Watson, that to bring our enquiry here was a long shot. I feared that I was theorizing beyond my data, but I seem to have been right.'

An Invitation

I am not, I hope, easily frightened, but before I fell asleep I could not forebear from reflecting that Holmes' 'long shot' had taken us from our accustomed purlieus of London to a remote Highland valley where total strangers sought to kill us. I hoped that his instincts were correct and that we would soon be able to unravel the London killings and the bizarre affair of the American angels.

We were at breakfast next morning when a rap sounded at the door. Mrs Mackintosh answered it and led in a roughly-clad young man, one who I recognized as having rowed the laird's boat to church on the previous morning. It crossed my mind that, even here, hundreds of miles from Baker Street, callers would seek out my friend. I was the more surprised when it was me that the youth addressed.

'Dr Watson,' he said, 'I'm Lacky Stuart, the laird's boatman. There's been an accident by the loch, and we'd be awfy grateful if you will come.'

'Is there no village doctor?' I asked, for I had no wish to trespass upon the territory of a professional colleague.

'Doctor Guthrie's awa' up the next glen,' said the lad. 'Mrs Drummond said you were a doctor.'

I made to rise from the table, but the youth forestalled me. 'Stay and finish your tea, Doctor. You needna' hurry. The man's deid anyway.'

Although there was no suffering patient awaiting me, I finished my tea quickly and trotted upstairs for my medical bag. Holmes followed the boy and I out on to the little jetty, where a small group of locals had gathered a few feet away from where a body lay sprawled face down on the planks. They parted silently and allowed Holmes and I to kneel beside the dead man.

The corpse was that of a stocky man in his middle years, dressed in the working clothing of the locality. At first I took him to be a victim of drowning, but when I turned him over it was immediately evident that the man had been murdered. A fresh wound showed where he had been stabbed forcibly below the ribs, the implement being driven upwards into the heart. I could find no other sign of any relevant injury upon him.

I sat back upon my heels. 'This man has

been murdered,' I told Holmes. 'He has been stabbed and fallen or been thrown in the loch.'

'Where did you find him?' Holmes asked Lacky Stuart.

'He was right here,' said the lad. 'He was floating beside the jetty when I came to my boat. I called a couple of folk to help me haul him out and we saw that he was deid.'

'Do you know who he was?' I asked.

'Aye. He was an American called Tam Chater. He's lived here a wee while.'

'The cold water will stop you estimating when he was killed,' Holmes observed to me. He turned to the onlookers. 'Did any of you see Tam Chater last night?' he asked them.

There was a muttered conference among them, then a voice called out, 'He was in the tavern last night.'

'And was he with anyone in particular?' asked Holmes.

'Aye,' said our informant. 'He was with the Americans who are staying with Maggie Drummond. They were together all the night, until Jock Snetton shut up shop.'

'Did any of you see where he went at closing time?' my friend asked.

'They all three went oot together,' our witness said, 'but where they went I canna say. It's only yards to Maggie Drummond's or Tam Chater's lodging at Mary Macfarlane's.'

Holmes made a quick examination of the hands and feet of the dead man then stood up.

'This is undoubtedly murder,' he said, addressing the spectators. 'Do you have a policeman in the village?'

Heads were shaken, then young Lacky spoke. 'I'll tell the laird, sir. He will wire for a polisman and they'll send us somebody.'

An elderly man in formal clothes stepped between the crowd and introduced himself as the minister of Strathcullar kirk. 'If you can think of no objection, Mr Holmes, I shall have the deceased removed to the kirk until the authorities arrive.'

We thanked him and left, the knot of spectators breaking up behind us. Lacky dropped down the steps to his boat and cast off for the castle.

Mrs Mackintosh was agog when we returned.

'Is that right, what Lacky said, that there's a man deid?'

'I'm afraid so,' I confirmed. 'The man you named to us last night, the American Tam Chater, has been murdered.'

'Murdered!' she exclaimed on a rising note. 'That canna be! There's no been a murder in Strathcullar since the days of the redcoats.'

'Then I regret all the more that I have to confirm Dr Watson's view,' Holmes said.

Our landlady looked from one to another of us owlishly. 'Och, the puir body,' she said. 'To be murdered so far frae his hame. Sit ye doon, gentlemen, and I'll mash you some fresh tea.'

By the time she returned, a new aspect of the affair had struck Mrs Mackintosh. 'Are ye saying that puir Tam was killed by someone in Strathcullar?' she asked, as she poured the tea.

'I fear that is very likely,' said Holmes.

'Lord save us!' she exclaimed. 'I dinna ken what the laird'll think of this. There's been nae murder in Strathcullar since the redcoat days.'

She withdrew to her kitchen, muttering to herself about the wickedness of the world, and Holmes and I drank our tea in silence for a while.

After a little while Holmes took out his cigarette case and offered it. 'Well, Watson,' he said, 'what do you make of this development?'

'At the most callous,' I said, 'it appears to indicate that we have an unknown ally in the village who is prepared to eliminate someone who attempted to shoot us.'

'That is a very simplistic explanation, Watson,' he said.

'You have reminded me often, Holmes, that the simplest answer is often the best.'

'So it may be – if it fits the facts, but we do not have enough facts to determine where your theory fits.'

'What further facts do you require?'

'I have pointed out to you that we are in danger in this place and my warning was underlined by Chater's attempted ambush yesterday. The information we lack and that endangers us every minute is a precise knowledge of what factions are involved in this matter and with what interest.'

'I do not follow you,' I admitted.

He heaved a sigh. 'Let me explain, Watson. At the outset there were Carter and Mc-Nair. Carter's intentions we know – they were to recover the French gold if possible and keep it out of the hands of the American conspirators. McNair, we have deduced, either had possession of the gold or knew where it could be found, and sought to enter into a trade with Carter. There arises the first problem. We do not know if McNair acted alone or in conjunction with another or others, and we cannot be sure that the motive was purely profit.'

'Surely it was!' I protested.

'You may well be right, Watson, but at present we cannot be sure. Whatever Mc-

Nair's motive it led someone to kill both him and Carter. I think we are agreed that the killer was the same man in both cases?'

I nodded and he continued.

'Those killings lead us into deeper water. On whose behalf was the killer acting? Was he merely someone who wished to prevent the United States government from laying hands on the gold? Was he one of the American conspirators? Or did he act from motives at which we can only guess?'

He paused to light another cigarette. 'The same kind of questions arise around the death of Tam Chater. Why did he attack us? Was he a functionary of the American conspiracy or did he have some other interest? Why has he now been killed – because he attacked us, or because he failed? Or was it for some reason totally unconnected with our enquiry? I doubt that last proposition, Watson, but we cannot rule it out entirely. The alarming fact is that we do not know how many factions are involved in this matter, nor who supports which. What we do know is that one or more of them will kill and appears to be adept in the use of a knife.'

He stopped and shook his head. I had rarely seen him look so serious at the prospects of danger in a case, nor known him warn me so severely.

After a moment I said, 'What are you proposing to do next?'

'Acquire more data, Watson, that is imperative – if only to lessen our own danger. With that in mind I propose that we take a stroll after dinner and visit the Strathcullar Inn.'

I was surprised to note that it was still full daylight when we made our visit to the inn, until I recollected how far north we were and that the summer was advancing.

Holmes stepped out ahead of me, his eyes fixed to the ground as though searching. We were a few doors from our destination when he swung his stick at something on the cobblestones.

'Aha!' he exclaimed. 'I thought there should be traces and here they are.'

I followed his pointing stick and saw small traces of what was undoubtedly blood on the cobbles. Holmes turned to the adjacent cottages, which were separated by a narrow pathway.

'The mouth of that entry would have been pitch dark when Chater left the inn last night, Watson. Let us examine it.'

We stepped into the narrow space, barely wide enough for two men to stand alongside each other, and my friend scanned the ground keenly.

'This is definitely where the attacker lay in

wait,' he said after a while. 'Here is where he knocked out his pipe as he waited. The tobacco is not American. Here are his footmarks; though there is no limp he is nevertheless a large man.'

'Why is there not more blood?' I asked.

'Because he killed with one savage thrust of the knife, then left it in the wound until he had the body at the waterside. No serious quantity of blood would have flowed until he removed the weapon, and by then he was dropping his victim in the loch. For the same reason, it is unlikely that the perpetrator's clothing will have been stained.'

He looked about him once more then stepped back into the street.

'I do not like it, Watson,' he remarked.

I raised my eyebrows interrogatively.

'The knife,' he explained. 'We know that Carter was killed by a thrown skean-dhu – an unusual and extremely skilful act in itself – and that McNair was killed by a blow from the same knife at close quarters. Now Chater is dead and a very similar weapon was used – as it was designed to be – at short range.'

'Then,' I suggested, 'we can be sure that there is in Strathcullar a killer whose chosen weapon is the skean-dhu and who handles it with deadly expertise.'

'That is what bothers me, Watson. If the

villagers were given to murder – and I gather from Mrs Mackintosh that they are not – they would use a weapon with which they are familiar.'

'But the skean-dhu is a Highland weapon,' I pointed out.

'So it is,' he agreed, 'but nowadays it is merely a decorative adjunct to Highland formal dress. It is not carried as a weapon or a tool. The knife with which the villagers are familiar will be a hunting knife – a tool, not a weapon – carried when hunting in order to skin and gralloch a deer. When it comes to murder I would have expected their weapon of choice to be a firearm. The knife is more redolent of the sailor or the Continental than of the Highland hunter.'

We made our way to the Strathcullar Inn, which turned out to be the last building in the row fronting the lochside, built of the same stone as the villagers' homes, but larger. Inside it was furnished with plain wooden chairs and tables with an occasional settle here and there. It occurred to me that the proprietor of such a house had little need to cosset his customers when he had no competition for miles in any direction.

Our stepping into the bar caused a low muttering across the whole of the smoky, L-shaped room. It was evident that the entire village knew our identities and the landlord confirmed it by his greeting.

'Mr Holmes, Doctor Watson,' he hailed us. 'It's a pleasure to see you in my house and to have the opportunity of thanking you for what you did for puir Tam this morning,' and he pushed two glasses of whisky across the bar.

'Little enough we could do for him,' I remarked.

The landlord shook his head, agreeing, but went on, 'Still and all, ye were prepared to step aside from your holiday because our ain doctor wasnae here.'

'We are not on holiday,' said Holmes, so clearly that the entire company could hear him. 'We are here to look into the murder in London of the laird's agent, Mr McNair. I am told that murder is extremely rare in these parts and that being so, the death of Tam Chater by violence shortly after our arrival in Strathcullar strikes me as a matter in which we might interest ourselves as well.'

This time there was complete silence from the room. Strathcullar had already formed its opinion of our presence and Holmes had merely confirmed it.

'With that in mind,' continued Holmes, 'I was hoping to see Red Ewan Breck here tonight.'

'He's here,' said our host. 'He's in the wee

back parlour with his other friend, Seamus the ganger. You'll find the door just right of the bar.'

'Thank you,' said Holmes, picking up his glass. 'Be so good as to send them through a drop of their own refreshment and two more of this excellent malt for Watson and myself.'

We made our way into the little parlour, which was slightly less utilitarian than the main bar. Two elderly men were seated together by the room's only table, both of them tall. One of them was round-faced with grey curls and the other leaner with grizzled hair streaked with its erstwhile red. An elderly mongrel dog, as grey as its master, slept on the floor alongside the grizzled man. Both lifted their glasses as we approached their table.

'Good luck to you, gentlemen,' said the round-faced man.

'Thank you,' said Holmes. 'I was merely seeking a word with Ewan Breck about the unfortunate death of his friend Chater.'

The leaner man shook his head, sadly. 'The murder, you mean. My friend Tam was murdered. You'll be Mr Holmes, the English detective, then?'

'I am,' said Holmes. 'I am looking into the murder of your friend and wondered what you could tell me about him.'

'Aye, I'll tell you about Tam Chater. He was an American, frae Boston, but whatever his nation he was the finest man I ever met.'

'And where did you meet him?'

'I was away in America for years when I was a young man, and I met him there, many years ago. We both worked up in the northwest, as messengers and haulers for the Hudson Bay Company, and our trails often crossed. When they found gold in Alaska we both decided to try our luck and we went and worked a claim for a while, but it was verra hard work, all digging in mud and cold water all the time and only finding the odd pennyweight of gold.'

He picked up his glass with a shaky hand and gazed across it thoughtfully.

'He saved my life, Tam Chater did. I thought I was gone, but Tam saved me.'

'How did that come about?'

'Well now, when we gave up the gold panning we thought that there was more money to be made bringing into the gold camps the things that folks were needing, so we started sledging and trucking supplies into the Yukon. We were out one night with two sledges of goods, camped in the snow, both of us asleep in our wee tent.'

He took a thoughtful sip as he conjured up the recollection.

'I was woken up by a noise outside and I

thought someone was after our gear on the sledges. So, I crawled out of my tent with a pistol in my hand and went to the nearest sledge. I couldnae see anyone, but a moment later something hit me a great dint in the back and flung me in the snow. My gun went spinning and a great big grizzly bear fell on to me.'

'A grizzly!' I exclaimed.

'Aye, Doctor. That's when I knew I was gone. They're terrible beasts, four or five times the weight of a grown man and with fistfuls of razor claws, and there was I – wrestling it without even my wee pistol. I was sure I was a dead man.'

He sipped again.

'Then Tammy came out of the tent with a rifle. Another man would have been feared to shoot in case of hitting me, but Tam knelt there in the snow and lifted his gun and put a shot straight through that bear's head, despite the fact that me and the beast were wrestling and rolling all over.'

'Remarkable,' said Holmes. 'He was an excellent shot, then?'

'He was that. The finest shot I ever saw, and after shooting the bear he put me on one of the sledges and he took both the sledges on to the next staging post. The post manager's wife patched me up and pulled me through, though it was a long time. But if I'd been with anyone but Tam, I'd be dead the noo and buried in Alaska.'

Holmes nodded. 'And did Tam Chater return from Alaska with you?'

'No,' said the old man. 'When I was well from the injuries the bear did me I thought I'd had enough of the Wild West, so I came home to Scotland. I'd been here some time, working for the laird and doing a wee bit of ghillying for sportsmen. Then one day, who should come walking doon frae the eastern pass, whistling like he always did, but Tammy Chater. I couldnae believe my eyes, but he told me he'd fallen out with the law in America and decided to come and look me up in Scotland.'

'You would have been pleased to see him?' I suggested.

'I was that. I thought I'd never see him again and here he was, as large as life. He settled down here and took to the ghillying. He got very good at it, he knew every nook and cranny for miles and the Americans who come here sometimes seemed to like the idea of an American ghillie.'

'Did he have any enemies in the village, Mr Breck?' asked Holmes.

The old man stared at him in surprise. 'Enemies!' he exclaimed. 'He had nae enemies. He was a good friend to all was Tam, and some scoundrel murdered him and threw him in the loch like an unwanted fish. You find him, Mr Holmes, you find him and I'll help you hang him!'

He had become very excited during this last speech and now the tears ran down his long, weathered face.

'He was well-liked by everyone,' said the other old man. 'We were all good friends.'

'You knew Chater well?' asked Holmes.

'Almost as well as Ewan. I'm Seamus Fisher, they call me Seamus the ganger because I used to work the roads with navvies, and I'm an outsider to Strathcullar like Tam was, but I'd known him before I came here. I come from the Emerald Isle and as a boy, I went to sea. I was on the potato boats to Liverpool and then on the North Atlantic and that's where I met Tam Chater. We both had a couple of tours on the old *Atlantic Champion*, then I got tired of the sea and took to navvying.'

He took out a tin and rolled a cigarette.

'I came to Strathcullar as ganger when they made a decent road through the eastern pass some years ago. I loved the place, its so peaceful and private, and when I gave up the roads I came back here to settle down. I hadn't been here long when who should show up but me old shipmate Tammy Chater. Now there's a coincidence for you – us three old partners from far-flung parts of the world and its oceans coming together here in little Strathcullar.'

'Oh, indeed,' agreed Holmes, though I recalled his oft-repeated dictum that co-incidence is the willing handmaiden of the lazy mind.

'Were all of you in here last night?' Holmes enquired.

'No, sir,' said the Irishman. 'Ewan was at the castle on the laird's business and I was at home for an evening. Those that were in say that Tam was drinking with two American walkers who came here the same day you did, sir. They were asking him to take them out today.'

'And did he leave alone?' asked Holmes.

'So they say, that he went back to his lodgings about his usual time.'

'And he had no enemies?' persisted my friend.

'None at all,' said the Irishman. 'As Ewan said, Tam Chater was a friend of everybody in the village.'

'I thank you, gentlemen,' said Holmes and stood up. At the door he paused. 'I'm sure you can tell me,' he said, 'if Chater wore a watch?'

They stared at him, dumbfounded. Then Breck broke the silence. 'He never needit a watch,' he said. 'He'd been at sea so long he could always tell the time by the sun, and at night he could tell it by the stars. Sometimes, when we ghillied together, I would pull out my old pocket watch and Tam would tell me what it said before I had it out of my pocket. No – he never had a watch.'

The landlord confirmed that Chater had been in his bar the previous night, drinking with the two American visitors, and had left alone at his usual hour.

'Holmes,' I said, as we sauntered home along the lochside, 'do you really believe it to be a coincidence that Chater and Fisher and Breck all ended up here together?'

'Of course not!' he snapped. He sounded so irritable that I forbore to ask about the watch.

Mrs Mackintosh served our supper in a state of excitement, having first handed to Holmes a letter that had been delivered by Lacky Stuart. He slit the envelope with his pocketknife, read the enclosed note then passed it to me.

It was a single sheet of expensive paper, headed with a coat of arms. The text read:

James Czernowski-Stuart,
Laird of Strathcullar,
is pleased to invite
Mr Sherlock Holmes and
John H. Watson, MD,
to dine with him at Strathcullar Castle

at seven o'clock tomorrow evening. No reply is necessary unless this is inconvenient, otherwise my boat will await you at half past six.

'Well,' remarked Holmes, 'that solves the problem of seeking an interview with the laird.'

Dinner at Strathcullar Castle

True to the laird's invitation, Lacky Stuart tapped Mrs Mackintosh's door at a little before half past six the next evening. Our good landlady was still in a state of excitement that her visitors from London merited an invitation to dine with the laird.

We followed Lacky to the jetty and boarded his boat. He pulled away with strong strokes, and soon we were gliding across the loch to Czernowski-Stuart's ancient fortress. It was a perfect early summer's evening and the rippling waters of the loch gleamed gold under the westering sun.

Holmes gazed about him. 'Lacky,' he said, 'what are all those little islands around the shores of the loch?'

He pointed to where two of them stood up from the water close together, dark hummocks crowned with trees.

'Och, them,' said the youth, dismissively. 'They're what we call crannogs. They're not real islands at all. They say that the auld folk, back in the auldest times, used to make

103

them so they could be safe from their enemies. They'd put loads of rocks into the water a little way from the shore, then build their houses on top, so that naebody could get at them easily. I suppose its much like the laird's castle being built on an island.'

Holmes nodded. 'Does anyone do anything with the crannogs nowadays?' he asked.

'Och, no,' said the boy. 'There's just clumps of trees on them. Sometimes the sporting visitors go on them when they're after wildfowl, and when I was a wee yin we used to dive off them in summer. It was a kind of a race – to go all round the loch and dive from each of the crannogs.'

'And you never found any trace of the old people who lived on them?' I said.

'Oh, the minister has a wee bowl that Doogie Herd brought up when he dived from one of them. The minister says its older than the time of our Lord.'

'And do the young lads still swim about them?' asked Holmes.

'Oh, aye,' said our boatman. 'Ever since Doogie Herd got a few shillings frae the minister for his bowl they've been going at it every summer, but they've never found anything more.'

'No sunken treasures, then?' said Holmes lightly.

Lacky grinned at him.

'I'm afraid,' he said, 'someone's been telling you about the French gold.'

'And what is there to tell about it?' asked Holmes.

Lacky continued to grin as he rowed. 'It's an auld story that, long years ago, the laird's ancestor, Bonnie Prince Charlie, was living abroad, and had dealings with the American colonists who were going to have a war with the English. The prince is supposed to have set up a great big payment of gold from the French, to help the Americans, but it got lost.'

'Lost?' queried Holmes.

'Aye, lost. The story goes that it was sent overland through Scotland to prevent the Revenue or the Royal Navy laying hands on it. Somebody turned traitor and told the English and they sent soldiers after it. The auld folk say they camped about Strathcullar for weeks and they searched every nook and cranny, though I don't know how they'd know since none of them were alive to see it. They never found it, so they went back to Inverness at the end, wi'oot a penny.'

'And what do you think became of the gold?' asked my friend.

Lacky bestowed upon us that look which is appropriate to a youth informing his elders; one of judicious unconcern.

'Myself,' he said, 'I'm nae sure there ever was any gold, but if there was, I think the soldiers were too late and the gold got away tae America.'

With this pronouncement he drew our boat on to the foreshore of the island and led us up to the castle door.

'How shall we recall you?' I asked.

'Nae need,' he said, 'nae need. I'm aboot the laird's business, so I'll be here at the shore when you want to go home.'

Holmes pulled the sturdy iron bell pull that hung by the castle's door and somewhere within a bell chimed. In a moment we heard bolts being drawn on the inside and the door was pulled back to reveal Ewan Breck, dressed more formally than when we last saw him.

'Mr Holmes, Dr Watson,' he hailed us. 'Welcome to Strathcullar Castle. His Highness is awaiting you. Be so good as to follow me.'

Sherlock Holmes noted how Breck referred to his master and lifted an eyebrow at me but said nothing. We followed Breck through a panelled entrance hall and through a door into what was probably the castle's banqueting hall in its heyday. In this wide, lofty chamber our host stood waiting, clad in full Highland formal dress, including a kilt of the hunting Stuart tartan, a costume which made our sober London black look positively drab. On the wall above him a portrait of Bonnie Prince Charlie, larger than life, confirmed such a strong visual resemblance that there could be no doubt that we were in the presence of a Stuart of the royal line.

Our host stepped forward, extended a hand from a lace-ruffled cuff and welcomed us both warmly.

'If I may be so impolite as to deal with a small matter of business before we dine, gentlemen, perhaps you would wish to know that I wired the police at the news of poor Chater's death and have had confirmation that an inspector will arrive in Strathcullar tomorrow, accompanied, it seems, by an officer from Scotland Yard.'

'That will be Inspector Hopkins,' said Holmes. 'He has the conduct of the London investigation.'

The laird nodded. 'As I said, business can wait until we have dined. Let me, in the meantime, show you a few of my curiosities.'

He led us to one side of the room, where a row of ancestral portraits and other paintings hung above a battery of chests and display cases. Here were exhibited all manner of artefacts, many old and rare and all connected with Scotland's past or the Jacobite cause. Here was handsome glassware finely engraved with portraits of the Pretender; silverware with Jacobite inscriptions and much more. Both Holmes and I were surprised at the size and extent of our host's collection.

The laird chuckled at our expressions of amazement. 'You'll be thinking,' he said, 'that not so many years ago I would have been hauled away and locked up for possessing these items. Nowadays the Lord Lieutenant of the county dines with me and makes no complaint about my little family collection.'

'The English establishment does not, then, regard you as a threat to the peace and order of the Empire?' said Holmes.

The laird chuckled again. 'The Jacobite cause died on Culloden Moor a century and a half past. Here, let me show you something.'

He drew a slip of pasteboard from one of the cases and held it so that we could see it was an old-fashioned playing card with words written on it.

'There is the death of my family's cause,' he said. 'That is the nine of diamonds – the so-called Curse of Scotland. You'll have heard how, playing cards after the battle, the Duke of Cumberland used a card to scrawl this infamous order that the Scottish wounded should be killed. They say this is the very card. Oh, I know there are many in Scotland who pay lip service to my family's cause. They wear the white rose, they go to their Jacobite balls, they sing the old songs and they drink toasts to "the king over the water", though the nearest thing they have to a king over the water is me on my island. From time to time there are even hotheads who seek to encourage me to claim the thrones of Scotland and England.'

'And how do you answer them?' asked Holmes.

'I tell them that we are in an age of railway engines and the electric telegraph. No rebellious host would reach the border before being faced with the British Army and cut down with machine guns in a confrontation that would make Culloden look like a village brawl. Besides, the old Queen and King Edward are distant relatives of mine. I've no more wish to start a family quarrel than a civil war.'

A discreet cough sounded behind us and we turned to find Ewan Breck waiting on us.

'Mrs Herd wishes me to tell you, Laird, that dinner will be served in ten minutes.'

'Time to introduce you to a few more of my curiosities,' said our host. 'What do you make of this, Mr Holmes?'

He laid out on top of one of the cabinets a row of circlets of glass, each with a part of a person painted upon it, thus a face on one, a trunk upon another, legs on a third and so on.

'It's a child's game.' I said. 'You shuffle the discs into any order you like to create a curious or bizarre figure when you look through them.'

The laird shook his head, as did Holmes. 'No,' said Holmes. 'If I am right, it has a much more serious purpose. During the Elizabethan persecution of Catholics, a similar device was used by adherents of the old faith. A person who regularly received important secret messages would have such a device – usually painted on slices of transparent horn, each slice being numbered. He could then be sent a date and a series of numbers. By putting the pieces in the correct order he could reveal a picture of the person who would call upon him. That way he could be sure that he was dealing with a genuine emissary and not a government spy and the messenger need carry no credentials that would give him away if he were searched. I had no idea that the Jacobites used it also.'

Czernowski-Stuart chuckled. 'You forget, Mr Holmes, that the principal objection of the English to my unfortunate forebears was that they were Catholics.'

He drew us further along the chamber and directed our attention to a large painting on the wall. Now I do not pretend to have much understanding of art, but I will assert that it was the finest landscape that I have ever seen.

Some six feet wide, the picture hung in an ornate gilt frame. It portrayed Loch Strathcullar on a summer's evening, seen from about the position of the old Pictish stone on the eastern pass. All of the lake and the little village were shown, the islands and the castle. A westering sun lay beyond a distant mountain and the loch and the clouds above it were tinted gold by the sun's reflections. A painted label was attached to the frame, saying, 'Golden Reflections – Midsummer's Eve on Loch Strathcullar by Mungo Breck'.

We absorbed this beautiful work in silence for some minutes, then Holmes said, 'Mungo Breck? I have not heard of him.'

'Nor would I expect you to have done,' said our host. 'Apart from that lovely thing there are very few other paintings of his known and almost all of them are in other rooms of this castle. We must make an opportunity for you to see them all in due course.'

'I would welcome it,' replied Holmes. 'Was

he a local man?'

'Oh, aye,' said the laird. 'He was the son of the village blacksmith and wheelwright a century and a half ago. The minister taught him to read and his father taught him his crafts, but he soon outstripped anything that anyone else had taught him.'

'Why is he not better known?' asked Holmes.

'Because, I imagine, he lived in this remote place and disappeared while still a young man.'

'Disappeared?' I exclaimed.

'Oh, aye, Doctor. According to the legend, young Breck was much taken with the idea of the American colonies revolting – his father had been a prominent supporter of the Bonnie Prince, after all – and one day young Mungo packed his bundle and announced that he was bound for America. Off he went, and from that day to this no more was ever heard of him in Strathcullar.'

'What a waste of talent,' commented Holmes, and as he spoke a gong sounded softly.

'Ah, dinner!' exclaimed our host, and led us across the chamber to a beautifully laid and set table, where he showed us to our seats. In moments Ewan Breck appeared with a serving maid and waited upon us – as well, I may say, as I have been served in great hotels in London or on the continent.

While we were served Holmes raised a question.

'May I ask,' he said, 'what you accept as a correct form of address to one who is, at the very least, a royal prince? I have heard you referred to as "His Highness". Is that the form you prefer?'

The laird laughed. 'Czernowski–Stuart is a dreadful mouthful, even for a Gaelic speaker, and I would not inflict it upon an Englishman. Equally, I would not discomfort my cousin Bertie's loyal subjects by asking them to acknowledge my royalty. The ancient and honourable title of "Laird" is quite sufficient for me, my friends and my tenants. Only the most determinedly romantic address me as anything else.'

With that problem of etiquette resolved, we fell to.

Prince Charlie's Angels

When the final plates were removed from our table, the laird commanded Ewan Breck to 'Bring the tray!'

His faithful servant brought a circular metal tray to the table, loaded with glasses and a decanter of whisky. When he had filled the glasses – including, with his master's consent, one for himself – the laird drew our attention to the tray.

Circular in form, it bore a rimmed boss at its centre. It would have been a quite unexceptional tray but for the decoration that covered its surface. It was painted with a bizarre pattern of spots, specks and smears of colour, which orbited about the central boss as though the painter had laid the tray on the mechanism of a gramophone and daubed at it as it rotated. It was a singular thing in itself and the more so to be displayed in a room which was full of artefacts of great taste and craftsmanship.

Our host observed our puzzled faces with a quiet smile, then ordered Breck to 'Bring the portrait!'

Breck brought from the sideboard a polished silver cylinder with a small stand at one end. He placed it carefully on the central boss of the curious tray and stepped back.

Even Holmes was startled at the result. Now the orbital daubs of colour on the tray were reflected on the highly polished surface of the cylinder, and there they resolved into a perfect portrait of the Young Pretender, Bonnie Prince Charlie.

Czernowski-Stuart laughed aloud. Holmes, who loved a good conjuring trick, applauded gently. 'I take it,' he said, 'that this little miracle is another work of Mungo Breck?'

'It is. I don't know if he devised the trick, but it was to save Jacobite gentlemen from arrest if they were found drinking together. So long as the central cylinder was knocked over, there was no evidence of a subversive portrait or that they were drinking to an illegal toast.'

We chuckled and our host asked Breck to bring cigars. They came in a beautiful bronze box, enamelled with a small reproduction of the painting 'Golden Reflections'. Holmes exclaimed over the workmanship which was, of course, that of Mungo Breck.

'I believe,' said the laird, 'that Mungo Breck made this box for one of the ladies of my family, to keep her powders and paints in. As you can see, the inside of the lid is polished as a mirror. I have converted its use so that I may have an excuse to handle it and admire it the more often.'

We cut and lit our cigars and our host dismissed Ewan Breck and leaned back in his chair.

'We have dined,' he said, 'as well as Strathcullar could let us, for every item we have eaten has come out of this valley. If you are satisfied, gentlemen, then the whisky stands on the table with the cigars, and it is, perhaps, time to get down to business.'

We nodded, and he resumed.

'I understand, Mr Holmes, that your presence in Strathcullar arose in the first place because of the murders in London of the American Carter and my man of business, McNair.'

'You noted Carter's death,' commented Holmes, with a slight trace of surprise.

'Come now, Mr Holmes. We may be a long way from the seats of power, but we have the telegraph and the London newspapers reach us – eventually. It is clear that Scotland Yard believes the two deaths are connected and, presumably, you concur.'

Holmes nodded. 'I do. Might I ask if you

have any knowledge of the American – Carter?'

Our host shook his head. 'None at all,' he said. 'What was he? The press says merely that he was a former soldier in Britain on business. Do you know what business?'

There was a long pause, during which Holmes looked thoughtfully at the man at the head of the table, and I realized he was considering how far he might expose his hand.

'He was,' Holmes said at last, 'a kind of spy.'

'A kind of spy!' echoed our host. 'For whom?'

'That,' said Holmes, 'I am obliged not to tell you, but I'm sure you will be able to draw a reasonable inference as this conversation continues. Suffice it to say, as a beginning, that the deaths of Carter and McNair, together with the recent murder of Tam Chater, all seem to me to revolve about the same focus and that focus is in – or is intimately connected with – Strathcullar.'

The laird said nothing, but rose from his seat and went to one of his display cabinets. Taking something from a drawer, he came back to the table and rolled the object across the tablecloth towards Holmes.

It wobbled as it rolled, gleaming under the candle lights. At last it dropped flat in front of my friend and he picked it up, examined both sides of it and passed it to me.

I had seen that it was a gold coin, but now I could see that one side bore the florid decorations that were common on the old coin known as an 'angel', while the other side bore the unmistakable likeness of Prince Charles James Stuart.

'Mr Holmes,' said the laird, resuming his seat, 'throughout my life I have known the story of Prince Charlie's gold. More than one poor loon has come here and scrambled about the hills looking for it. Nobody has died because of it until now. What is this all about?'

'I must answer your question, Laird, with another. What do you know of the gold? Was it ever here? Is it here now?'

The laird refilled his glass and drew on his cigar. 'I lived in France for a while when I was young,' he said. 'Because of my ancestry and my historic interest, it amused me to try to find out about the famous gold. Through a contact in French government circles I was permitted access to certain records. From these I learned a few crucial facts. There certainly was such a payment agreed to the American rebels by the French and, so that France would not be blamed if it came to light, the gold was converted into those angel coins which my illustrious ancestor had minted. It was decided that shipment around the coasts of Britain was dangerous. To the south the shipment would be exposed to the search and seizures of the Royal Navy and the Revenue, to which the American colonists so objected. To the north there would be the added dangers of the route, weather and tides. So, it was planned to send the shipment directly, in an apparently neutral vessel, to Scotland, where Jacobite supporters would escort it to the west coast. There, an American-owned vessel, crewed by defecting Englishmen, would take the gold on board and run for America, hoping to avoid King George's Navy and his Revenue.'

He paused.

'But the gold never reached its destination?' queried Holmes.

'No,' said the laird. 'According to French spies in Scotland, the arrival of the gold was betrayed by an informer and the Army was sent to track it down. The Navy and the Revenue patrolled the west coast, searching anything that might be carrying the shipment, but it was never found. The Army concluded that the gold had disappeared somewhere about Strathcullar. They camped here and searched the hills and moors, dragged the lake, bribed everyone they thought might talk, but all to no avail. They found nothing.'

When Czernowski-Stuart had finished his tale Holmes drew a long breath.

'So,' he said, 'there was an enormous shipment of gold and it never reached America. It may well still be in this vicinity.'

'Aye,' agreed the laird, 'unless, of course, someone has taken it away in the meantime. Still, I imagine I would have come to know of that.'

'You asked,' said Holmes, 'why people are being murdered in the pursuit of that gold, Laird. You will, of course, be aware of the assassination of President McKinley last year.'

'Of course,' said our host, 'but what has the murder of America's president by a lunatic to do with a hoard of gold hidden in the wilds of Scotland?'

'Because those who set Czolgosz on to kill the president are among those who seek Bonnie Prince Charlie's gold.'

The laird stared at Holmes for a long moment, then drew furiously on his cigar.

'You mean that the president was the victim of a conspiracy, not a lone lunatic? Was Carter involved with the conspiracy?'

Holmes shook his head. 'No,' he said. 'The assassination was, indeed, the work of a conspiracy, whose intent it is to disrupt the government of the United States and, eventually, to seize the reins of power. Carter was one of those whose task it was to prevent this outcome.'

'And where do you come into this, Mr Holmes? For whom do you act?'

'Once again, Laird, I must refuse to reveal my client. My personal intention is to reveal the killers of Carter, McNair and now Chater. My client wishes me to determine whether there is a hoard of gold hidden hereabouts and, if so, locate it, so that it may be removed from the clutches of the American conspirators. I should assure you that those instructing me intend no harm to the government of Scotland, England or France. They merely seek to protect America against the harm that the gold would do in the wrong hands.'

The laird nodded. 'But why has all this come about now?' he asked. 'People have known the story of the gold for a century and more. We've had poor loons come here seeking it, wandering about the hills and rowing the lake. What has started the killing?'

'Somebody,' said Holmes, 'believed that he knew the whereabouts of the gold and tried to sell it to the Americans.'

'Who was that?' asked our host.

'Your man of business – McNair,' said Holmes. 'What do you know of the man?'

'McNair? He was a lowlander, from Edinburgh or thereabouts. He came to Inverness to take a partnership in an old firm called Libbett and Gibson, who have looked after the affairs of the Strathcullar estate for many years. The older partners were finding journeys out here a wee bit wearing, so they were glad to have a younger, active man to carry the estate's affairs and make any visits.'

'Did he come here often?'

'No so often, but he would stay here in the castle for a few days when he came. He was an affable enough fellow and I was pleased to have him at my table. He was well-read and had a romantic affection for Jacobite legends. He was one of those I talked about, who sing the old songs and wear the white rose.'

'Did he have much to do with people in the village?' asked Holmes.

'Aye. Most evenings after dinner he would have Lacky row him and Ewan Breck over to the inn, where he said he heard the most marvellous tales from the villagers. Sometimes he'd take a day off from his papers and go about the hills with Tam Chater.'

'So, he might well have been seeking the gold,' remarked Holmes. 'Tell me, Laird, as your man of business he'd have had access to any documents relating to the estate.

Could he have found something in them that led him to the location of the gold?'

Czernowski-Stuart smiled. 'I very much doubt it,' he said. 'My two old uncles were great antiquarians and pored over every scrap of paper and parchment in our archives. If it was there I would have backed them to find it. Why do you ask?'

'Because we know that McNair did come across some indication of the gold's whereabouts that he regarded as reliable. He was so sure of himself that he entered into correspondence with what he believed to be a representative of the American conspirators. How he made that contact in the first place we do not know – perhaps through Chater. It may be that Chater was always an agent of the Americans in seeking the gold, which would account for his desire to retire to Strathcullar.'

'If he was so dishonest,' said the laird, 'why did he not simply steal the gold?'

'Because he would have found it extremely difficult to dispose of such a quantity of Jacobite angels on this side of the Atlantic. Better to sell to the Americans at discount.'

'And how did this bring about his death?' asked our host.

'Because somebody became aware of his intentions – somebody who was determined that neither McNair nor the Americans should profit by the gold and so killed him and Carter.'

There was a point that had puzzled me for some time, so I asked, 'How did the Americans ever come to learn of the gold, Holmes?'

'Watson!' he exclaimed. 'It was intended for them in the first place. There will be records in America, as there are in France. As to how they suspected it's being hidden near Strathcullar, I suggest two possibilities – firstly that the painter Mungo Breck packed up and went to America as a messenger. More likely, I believe, is that Ewan Breck spoke carelessly of the matter while in North America and thus attracted the ears of treasure-hunting adventurers like Chater.'

'And how do you propose to unravel this matter, Mr Holmes?' asked the laird.

'If McNair could find the whereabouts of the gold, then so can I. What is possible for one man is always possible for another.'

The laird eyed him thoughtfully. 'I do not doubt your considerable skills, Mr Holmes, and I applaud your confidence in yourself, but you should consider that three men have been murdered recently over this matter. You do not know who are your enemies. Surely you will be a target?'

Holmes smiled. 'Since I do not know the

identity of my enemies, it behoves me to draw them into the open, and the best way to do that is to stay here in Strathcullar and go about my business until they attack me.'

I do not think that any of us imagined that the attack would come so soon.

Danger in the Dark

We lit fresh cigars, refilled our glasses and turned to lighter topics until it was time for us to leave. Our host walked us to the door and stood with us, breathing in the fresh night air.

It was a moonless, warm night, with not a breath of wind. The waters of the loch were as black as oil and the far shore could scarcely be discerned against the dark sky. By the jetty the faithful Lacky slept under a boat cloak in the stern of his vessel, a small lantern lighted and hanging from the prow. As we reached the boat he helped us aboard and was soon pulling out into the almost impenetrable blackness with every confidence.

'Do you always carry a lamp at night?' asked my friend.

'Oh, aye,' replied the boy. 'It lets folk on shore or on the island see whereabouts I am at night, if I'm coming or going. Then, when the visitors are here for the wildfowl and hanging about the crannogs and the shore, it tells them where I am and stops them shooting at me.'

We laughed and sat in silence as he pulled us towards the jetty. A few strokes and a neat manoeuvre of the oars then the lantern showed us that Lacky had placed us immediately beside the steps up to the jetty.

Holmes rose and picked up his stick. I gathered myself to follow him, but I have never been entirely easy in small boats since my injury. As I straightened myself the vessel shifted, rocking slightly under our feet. Holmes stooped, securing his balance by placing a hand on a thwart. As he did so, something whirred through the darkness from above and struck the thwart, only inches from Holmes' outstretched hand.

Holmes sprang for the jetty steps and ran up them, while I made as fast as I could behind him. Lacky followed us up. Above us we heard footsteps running away along the timbers of the jetty.

My friend reached the top of the steps and gave chase, though it was so dark that we could not even see the far end of the jetty. I ran blindly, following Holmes' steps and the sound of those that he was following.

Suddenly Holmes stopped dead and spun around, spreading his long arms wide, so as to catch Lacky and myself as we came up to him. As we did so I realized that I could no longer hear our attacker's running footsteps.

Holmes had realized, as I had not, that the sound of running feet had ceased because our attacker had jumped ahead, leaping for the shoreward end of the jetty.

'A match, Watson!' commanded Holmes. 'A match!'

Quickly I fumbled my vesta case from my pocket and struck one. Holmes took it from my fingers and held it high. It made little impact upon the surrounding darkness, its pale flame hardly reaching the jetty's end, but it was sufficient to show us the trap that had been prepared for us. The last two planks of the jetty had been levered away, leaving a yawning gap at the landward end. Impelled by our resentment of the knife attack, blinded by the dark night, we would certainly have run into the trap but for Holmes' rapid ability to interpret the sounds he had heard.

I was still gaping at the trap that had been prepared for us when Holmes said, 'Do you have your pistol on you, Watson?'

'No,' I replied. 'I did not think it necessary to carry it on a social visit to dine with the local landowner.'

'A pity,' he said, tersely. 'Perhaps in future you will bear the idea in mind. We are not in our accustomed social circles here.'

We made our way to the cobbled roadside,

stepping cautiously along the lateral members of the jetty. Lacky looked back and remarked that he would have little trouble fixing the damage in the morning. Holmes slipped him a coin and asked him to take us to the little graveyard island when he had finished repairing the jetty.

'That's Inish Beg,' said the lad. 'The island with the castle is Inish Mor – the great island – and the wee island is Inish Beg. Do you really wish to visit there, sirs? There's nothing there except graves and an old chapel building.' The youth seemed uncharacteristically reluctant.

'Surely you're not afraid of the dead on Inish Beg?' I asked.

'It's no' a good place,' he asserted. 'Anyone in Strathcullar will tell you there's bogles and ghosts there. It's not a Christian place – the folk who made it were heathens.'

'Nevertheless,' said Holmes, 'we would like to see these ancient burials. Perhaps you will be good enough to tap Mrs Mackintosh's door once the jetty is repaired.'

We returned to our lodgings, where our good landlady was awaiting us, agog with expectation of tales of wonder from the laird's castle. She was disappointed at the news that the laird's dinner service was not of solid gold.

'Kirsty Hudson says that you're a man

that knows all sorts of things, Mr Holmes,' she said. 'Do ye think that the laird really is the rightful King of Scotland and England?'

'I cannot say,' replied Holmes, 'that succession to the throne is a matter which has much engaged me. I am content, as a rule, to accept the generally acknowledged and crowned monarch and attempt to do my duty by them. Your laird may have a claim to the crown, but then I recall a Welsh gentleman who used to address the crowds at Hyde Park Corner with claims that he was the last of the Tudors and thereby our lawful king. If he was correct, and is still extant, then he would, presumably, take precedence over a Stuart.'

Mrs Mackintosh looked crestfallen at the idea of a Welsh king, and applied herself to serving our tea before retiring and leaving us to consider the evening's events.

Holmes lit his meerschaum and sprawled in his armchair with an expression of satisfaction.

'A useful expedition, I think, Watson,' he remarked.

'Useful!' I exclaimed, for I was still disturbed by my recollection of events at the lochside. 'You came infernally near getting stabbed by a maniac!'

'There,' he said, 'you are wrong on at least two points. Had our killer really intended to

stab me as I left the boat he is quite sufficiently skilled to have done so. That, however,
would have been too similar to the death of
Chater. As it was, he attempted to lure us
into a trap which might, afterwards, have
been seen as an accident. If he had replaced
the missing timbers before dawn, you,
Lacky and I would have become the victims
of a mysterious accident.'

'Nevertheless,' I grumbled, 'I believe you
are taking the dangers of our situation
altogether too lightly, Holmes.'

He chuckled. 'Let me remind you, Watson,
that it was I who warned you of the especial
dangers of this inquiry. You heard me set out
my intentions to the laird. There is really no
other way to proceed. We cannot defeat our
opponents until we know their identity. Tonight has been useful in part by eliminating
one possible suspect.'

'Really?' I said.

'I had considered,' said Holmes, 'that Red
Ewan might be the killer of Carter and
McNair. He is, it seems, a loyal supporter of
the laird. If he is one of those romantic Jacobites who believe that a Stuart on the throne
is still a possibility, he might have wished to
preserve the prince's gold for such a purpose and prevent McNair or Carter disposing of it.'

'True,' I agreed, 'but his eyesight is failing,

unless I miss my diagnosis, and his hand shakes. He was not the thrower of that knife in Regent's Park.'

'Certainly,' said Holmes, 'and his affection for the late Chater did not seem to me to be feigned. However, tonight has eliminated him completely. When we were attacked, Red Ewan was tucked up in his quarters on Inish Mor. We must look elsewhere.'

'Have you any other ideas?' I asked.

'Oh, indeed. I am inclined to look with suspicion on the Irishman.'

'Seamus the ganger?' I said.

Holmes nodded. 'Seamus Fisher. He is of the right physical type, he is a former seaman which may have made him adept with a knife, and he seems, like Chater, to have retired to Strathcullar for the most flimsy of reasons.'

It was my turn to nod. 'But why would he be involved?' I queried.

'It is,' said my friend, 'a reasonable assumption that the motive in any case is the acquisition or preservation of the French gold. Carter, we know, sought to find it for the American government; McNair, it seems, sought to dispose of it to the American conspirators for profit. Their killer prevented both of them, perhaps because he wished to ensure that the conspirators acquired the gold without McNair's intervention. On the other hand, the killer may have other purposes for the hoard – he may desire it for himself or he may wish to apply it to some other purpose. It could be Fisher and he may be seeking merely to feather his own nest.'

I considered his arguments. 'What about Seamus's name?' I asked. 'He appears to have a name like "Dougherty" or "Flaherty" tattooed on his right forearm.'

Holmes laughed. 'I am pleased to note,' he said, 'that I have taught you over the years to be observant of tattoos – though not, it seems, sufficiently observant.'

'When we met him at the inn,' I said, 'I especially noted that he had the letters "E–R–T–Y" tattooed on a scroll on his right forearm. I took them to be part of a name. I could make no other sense of them.'

Holmes laughed again. 'People rarely have their own names tattooed about their persons. If it were a name, it might well be the name of a sweetheart, but it was not a name. Did you see what lay above the scroll?'

'No,' I admitted.

'I glimpsed,' said Holmes, 'the same letters, but above them appeared the tip of a knife, dripping blood.'

'A knife!' I exclaimed.

'Precisely, Watson. A killer's knife. The

letters, if you had observed more closely, had a gap between the "R" and the "T". So far from being a sweetheart's name, they spell out a revolutionary slogan.'

'You mean that Fisher is a Fenian or something of that ilk?'

He shook his head. 'No. It was not *"Erin Go Bragh"* or any slogan of the Fenian Brotherhood. It was *"Sic Semper Tyrannis".*'

I was bewildered for a moment, then the reference came to me. *'Sic Semper Tyrannis* – thus always with tyrants. But that,' I said, 'was what...'

Holmes raised a hand and forestalled me. 'Precisely,' he said. 'It was what our former client Booth* is said to have shouted from the stage of Ford's Theatre after killing President Lincoln.'

I was silent again for a moment. 'Then,' I said at last, 'Fisher carries an American slogan which refers specifically to the death of a president.'

Holmes smiled. 'Seamus Fisher may have come to Strathcullar with a road gang in all innocence, but here he met again his old seagoing chum Chater, a treasure hunter. If he learned of Tam Chater's business in the village, it may have occurred to him that the

*See *Sherlock Holmes and the Royal Flush*, Constable & Co, 1998.

gold would be better employed about his fellow-conspirators' business than taken by Chater.'

'Then, if he and Chater were working together, why has he killed Chater?'

Holmes drew on his pipe. 'I did not say that they were working together. Fisher may have pretended to collaborate with Chater, or he may merely have watched him to see what Chater discovered. The person who stabbed Chater, if it was Fisher or not, searched his clothing for something.'

'How do you know that?' I asked, astonished.

'When you examined Chater's corpse, Watson, you failed to note that the inside watch pocket of his old jacket was turned inside out, as though it had been quickly rifled. You heard it confirmed that Chater never carried a watch, but a watch pocket is a handy repository for small items one does not wish to lose. Ergo, somebody searched his body and may have taken something from him. That person was most probably Fisher.'

'What do you think they took?' I asked.

'I do not know that they took anything. I said only that they searched for something. I imagine that they believed that Chater carried some clue to the whereabouts of the gold.'

'Why, then, do you think that Chater was killed?'

'I believe that Chater saw himself as well on the way to achieving his goal. Our sudden arrival in Strathcullar disturbed him. It may have set him at odds with Fisher, if they were indeed co-workers. His response was to attempt to kill me or to frighten us away. Fisher may have regarded that as a mistake – either that Chater tried to kill me, or that he failed. Whether Fisher intends the gold for the American conspirators or for himself, he would need to eliminate Chater at some point, so he may have reasoned that he should kill Chater and take whatever the American knew.'

This was very deep for me and I said so. 'But you regard this evening as having been useful?'

'Oh, indubitably,' he replied. 'Apart from eliminating a possible suspect, we have been able to confirm what we did not know when first we came here – that there really was a shipment of gold from France to revolutionary America; that the English failed to seize it and that it may well still be in this vicinity. All of that is invaluable additional data. Now, I suggest that we retire and see what further data the official police bring from Inverness tomorrow.'

The Island of the Outcast Dead

Our slumbers were interrupted early on the next morning by the sound of vigorous hammering from the jetty. A glance from our window revealed young Lacky hard at his repairs.

'Come, Holmes,' I said. 'Lacky has nearly done his work and will soon call for us. We must be at breakfast.'

We had, in fact, just completed our meal when our boatman tapped the door and enquired for us. Mrs Mackintosh had prepared provisions for our little expedition and we were soon clambering aboard the boat.

So far from the previous night's voyage across an oleaginous black loch, the day was warm and sunny and the water around us reflected a bright blue sky. But for the grim nature of our destination and the knowledge that at least one person in Strathcullar was trying to kill us, I might have looked forward to a pleasant day.

Holmes lit his pipe as we pulled away, and

began asking our conductor about the little island.

'Well, the dominie and the minister both say that it goes back to the first people who was ever in Strathcullar. They say that the old folk who lived on the crannogs are buried there – the same folk that put the big stone up on the eastern pass. Some of the gravestones on Inish Beg have got weirdy animals cut on them, like you'd never see in Scotland. Some of them have no stone at all, just a lump of rock. I wouldnae like to be buried like that. I'd like a proper headstone with my full name – Gordon Lachlan Stuart – and the dates I lived and the fact that I was boatman to the King of Scotland. The minister sees that anyone who's buried there noo gets a stone, whoever he was, but I'm going to be buried in the kirkyard, not on Inish Beg.'

'And who gets buried there now?' asked Holmes.

'Puir mad folk that have done away with themselves, for one. The minister says that it is a great sin and people who do it cannae be buried in the kirkyard, they must go to Inish Beg because that was never Christian ground.'

'And are there many suicides in Strathcullar nowadays?' I asked.

'Losh, no, Doctor! It's a fine, healthy place

to live, but it can get a wee bit hard on the auld folk in the middle of winter and sometimes one of them will put themselves away to be out of it. Old Cathy Gordon did last winter, but she was crazed anyway. There was a lot in the village as said that the minister was being too hard, making her lie on Inish Beg, that she was a puir crazed old soul who didnae know any better, but he insisted.'

He paused a while, then resumed his narrative. 'Some of the graves on the island have stones with no names because naebody ever knew who they were.'

'And how did those burials come about?' asked Holmes.

'Mostly they're from the old days – the troubled times wi' the redcoats and all that. There was a deal of murdering going about in Scotland in them days, and folk would be found dead on the hills, or in the loch, and naebody would know if they were English or Scots. The minister at the time was a good King's man, and he wouldnae have strangers buried in the kirkyard in case they were English. He believed that the English had proved they were no Christians by their actions in Scotland, and he wouldnae risk having them in his kirkyard – begging your pardon, gentlemen.'

We laughed to ease the lad's embarrassment at his story, and Holmes commented drily, 'Then we must make sure, Watson, that we do not die in Strathcullar and end our days among the rejected dead on Inish Beg.'

'Someone tried to kill you last night,' remarked Lacky. 'Moving those boards wasnae a joke. Somebody meant you to fall on to the rocks below the jetty, or to go into the loch. You'd have been in a sad case in the dark last night.'

'So they did,' agreed Holmes. 'Have you any idea who it was and why they did it?'

'Why they did it?' echoed the boy. 'There's a lot of folk in the village who think you're here tae find the French gold for the English government. They think that if there's gold about, it's oor gold, Scottish gold. They reckon that the laird should have the gold and he'd have a chance of making himself king.'

Holmes smiled sadly. 'Your laird is a good man, Lacky,' he said, 'and whatever his ancestry, he has no wish to be the King of Scotland, England or both. He wishes only to be a good laird to his people in Strathcullar.'

'Aye,' agreed the lad, ruefully. 'I ken you're right,' and I saw the vision of revolt flicker out of his eyes. 'But there are plenty in the village who think that's why you're here.'

'You may tell them,' said Holmes, 'that I am not working for the English government, and if I should find the gold it will not be on England's behalf.'

'Very good, Mr Holmes,' said the lad, and swung our boat against the narrow shingle beach that rimmed Inish Beg.

We were soon ashore and looking about us. Holmes pointed suddenly to the village on the shore. 'Look!' he said. 'The trap from the railway has arrived at the jetty. That will be the official police from Inverness and they will wish to see the laird. You may leave Watson and me here, Lacky, and row them across, then come back for us. There's no need to hurry. We shall be some time here.'

The lad nodded and took up his oars again. 'While you're on Inish Beg,' he said, 'make sure you see the tinkers' stones.'

'What are they?' asked Holmes.

'They're stones that was put up over the grave of a whole family of tinkers – gypsies, you'd call them. They came to Strathcullar years ago and camped on the other side of the loch because the folk wouldnae let them into the village. Then they all died in their camp. Folk reckoned that they'd been in one of the towns and caught some fever or something and they wouldnae have them buried in the kirkyard because of the infection.'

'But there were stones put up?' commented Holmes.

'Oh, aye,' said the youth. 'You ken Mungo
Breck who painted that braw picture of the
loch that the laird has? They say he carved
the headstones himself. That's why I telled
you to look at them.'

With a wave of the hand he was gone,
pulling strongly towards the distant jetty.

I looked about us again. Inish Beg was
small, only about a hundred yards across.
Inside the shingle beach that rimmed the
entire island, a tumbledown wooden fence
surrounded the graveyard and within that
were the remains of an ancient stone wall.

'What a strange place,' I said, 'with strange
customs.'

'Neither the island nor the local customs
are so very strange,' replied Holmes. 'I have
seen similar burial areas in Ireland and I
believe that there are some in East Anglia.
Christians, as you know, believe in burying
their dead in hallowed ground. A pagan
graveyard they regard as unhallowed, so it
serves as a useful depository for those whom
they would not wish to have in their own
graveyard. It has its own logic.'

We walked to the stone wall, and Holmes
pointed out where two narrow entrances
through the wall flanked a kind of large
table set into the wall.

'For the convenience of the bearers,' he remarked, 'so that they did not have to struggle with lifting a coffin across the wall. Here they can rest their burden on the big flat stone, pass through the entrances in the wall and take up the coffin again from the other side. Again, I have seen similar in Ireland.'

I had not looked forward to our visit to Inish Beg, feeling that there were better ways of passing a sunny day in the Highlands than examining an ancient graveyard, but as we strolled about the little enclosure I found much that fascinated me.

As Lacky had told us, there were many small mounds that bore no stone at all, and some with only an uncarved stump of rock, but here and there were stones carved with the writhing animals and flowing decorations of Pictish ornament. Among the more modern memorials were stones to suicides, and more than a few with no name, merely 'A stranger found dead at Strathcullar' and a date, usually from the time of the Jacobite uprisings.

Apart from burials, there seemed to be nothing on Inish Beg save a small stone building with doors at each end and one window by the front door. Examination of it showed that it contained nothing except a crude stone table.

'It will be to rest a coffin on while the occupant is "waked",' commented Holmes. 'The Celts believe very strongly that a dead body must be always watched until it is properly interred, in case the devil should steal away the soul.'

We came at length to what Lacky had called the 'tinker stones', a row of six headstones in a line. It would take a more authoritative eye than mine to determine that the hand of Mungo Breck had cut the stones, but the inscription and decorations on them were certainly cut with considerable skill and worthy of a better display than on this remote island of the rejected dead.

Each stone bore a similar text – 'An Egyptian wanderer, known to God, who died at Strathcullar of an unknown fever, 1775'. Above each inscription was a decoration consisting of a winged angel's head, from which depended fruit, flowers and sprays that filled much of the stone.

'Apples!' I exclaimed.

'You think them unusual, Watson?' said Holmes. 'Not here in the Highlands. You forget that our Celtic forebears believed in a blessed other world beyond the Western Ocean, a land of apple trees where the honoured dead might enjoy eternity. It seems that our artist believed that these poor wanderers should end their travels with something better than a miserable death from fever in a remote valley in the Highlands.'

I nodded and we continued our strolling. From time to time I noted that my friend drew out his watch and glanced at the sky. After a while I said, 'Are you anxious about the time? Lacky will not strand us here.'

'Not at all,' he said. 'I was merely observing the movement of the sun.'

'It has been done,' I joked. 'It moves that way,' and I swung my stick in a wide arc.

'So it does,' he said, 'so it does, and that is what puzzles me.'

I was about to question his curious response when a bright flash caught my eye. I looked and saw it again.

'Holmes,' I said, 'someone is watching us through glasses.' I drew his attention to where I had seen the flash, above and behind the cottages on the lochside.

Holmes watched for a while. 'You are right,' he said at last. 'Someone is on the hillside, watching this island.'

'You do not think,' I asked, 'that someone might try a rifle shot?'

Holmes curled his lip. 'It would be a very long shot,' he opined, 'even for a skilled marksman. Besides, the person with the glasses is only just beyond the village. If he fired a shot he would certainly be heard and might be apprehended or at least identified. I would have thought that any such attempt would be better made from the other side of the loch. But cheer up, Watson. Here comes our boat.'

The Official Police

Lacky had us back to our lodgings in ample time for tea, served on Mrs Mackintosh's usual generous scale.

We had just retired to the sitting room with a pot of tea when our hostess came to inform us that we had visitors. These turned out to be Stanley Hopkins and a uniformed colleague, a stocky, grizzled man who was introduced as Inspector McBrain from Inverness.

Once the tea was served, Holmes opened the discussion.

'Well, Hopkins,' he said, 'what have you learned in Inverness?'

'With the help of my Scottish colleagues, I have managed to learn a lot about Mr McNair.' He pulled a notebook from his pocket. 'Do you want his background, Mr Holmes?'

'I have been starved of data in this matter since the beginning,' claimed Holmes. 'Any least crumb that you can offer will be welcome. Fire away.'

'Well, then, it seems that McNair was a lowlander, being the son of a large-scale farmer in the Lothians. He studied law at Edinburgh and passed well as a Writer to the Signet. When he had put in a few years' practise with a commercial firm in Edinburgh, he purchased a junior partnership in an old established business in Inverness. The police at Edinburgh could not prove anything against him, but they have indicated that he may have left Edinburgh leaving serious debts behind and that there could have been something a bit irregular in the way he financed his purchase of the Inverness partnership.'

He paused and sipped his tea.

'Nevertheless,' he continued, 'the partners in Inverness were ageing and wanted young blood. They seem to have been pleased to acquire his services and pleased by the results.'

'You have, of course, interviewed them?' said Holmes.

'Oh, aye,' said Inspector McBrain. 'Inspector Hopkins and I spent a deal of time in their chambers.'

Holmes nodded and waved to Hopkins to carry on. 'As you know, Mr Holmes, the Laird of Strathcullar was a client of that firm – indeed, the estate had been looked after by the same firm for generations. The old boys were getting a bit past dragging themselves out here to attend to the laird's matters and were glad of a younger partner who seemed to enjoy his visits to Strathcullar. They let him have the entire conduct of the laird's matters, and it seems he conducted them very well.'

'Were there,' asked my friend, 'any other matters in which McNair did less well?'

Both officers shook their heads. 'No, Mr Holmes,' replied McBrain. 'McNair having been murdered, we asked his former partners to re-check every matter that he had handled since he joined them. They were satisfied that he had conducted his clients' affair properly and expeditiously, apart from one wee thing.'

Holmes' eyes gleamed. 'And what was that, Inspector?'

'I don't know exactly what you might call it. It isnae crime, but it seems to me to be a wee bit too sharp for a professional man. He seems to have made a practise of profiting by information given him in confidence, taking advantage of knowing what others didnae to turn a few guineas.'

'And why do you think that was?' asked Holmes.

'Because he was almost always in debt,' said Hopkins. 'He carried on an energetic social life. Soon after he came to Inverness he made himself known to the city's society by joining all the best clubs and organizations. He was out every night, at balls and soirées. Although he was lowland born, he became a leading light of the city's Jacobite Society, often to be seen in full Highland dress.'

'He was not, I take it,' enquired Holmes, 'a genuine revolutionary, who would replace King Edward with the Laird of Strathcullar?'

'Losh, no,' said the inspector. 'He was one of those fancy romantics, who like the dress and the songs and the stories. He spent a lot of time looking into old legends and tales of the Risings. The laird here has told us this afternoon that he was the same when he came here – digging about in the castle's archives and spending evenings in the inn, chatting with the old folk about the Jacobite times.'

'And why do you think that was?' persisted my friend.

'When we first discussed this matter, Mr Holmes,' said the Scotland Yarder, 'you said that you believed that there was a Jacobite connection.'

Holmes nodded. 'And you – and Watson – treated me as if I had taken leave of my senses.'

'I apologise,' said Hopkins. 'I believe that

McNair, whether he had debts from his Edinburgh days or not, built up debts by his socializing and card-playing in Inverness. At the same time he posed as a romantic Jacobite enthusiast because it gave him access to some of the best Inverness society. In the course of that, he came across the story of Prince Charlie's gold. To a man with his debts and his eye on the main chance it would be a magnet. If he finally discovered where the gold was, he could not steal it and market it without attracting attention, but somehow he came into contact with the American, Carter, and was proposing to sell the secrets of the gold's whereabouts; a much safer proposition.'

'Not, as it transpired,' remarked Holmes. 'Though he could hardly have realized the extraordinary web that has grown around the search for the French gold, nor that Carter was not what he seemed.'

'What exactly was Carter?' asked Hopkins.

'You may take my word for it that Carter was acting in the full knowledge of the United States government. It was their intention that, whoever laid hands on the gold, it should not be the cadre of plotters who brought about the murder of President McKinley.'

'But the president was assassinated by a

lone lunatic,' protested McBrain.

'So we are told by American governmental sources,' agreed Holmes, 'but how much does that mean? Is any modern state going to admit to the world that a powerful conspiracy is afoot within its borders, determined to overthrow the republic and that it has already succeeded in removing the head of state? I think not. The United States is a young country, but within a short time of its foundation Washington was having to put down internal revolt. In a few years more there was Burr's rebellion, for which he was lucky not to be executed. We are all old enough to recall the special horror of their Civil War. Civil wars breed a particular resentment. The social, economic and political differences between the former Union and Confederacy strike me as an excellent breeding ground for discontent and malice. Poor Carter's business was to stop those elements getting their hands on the Strathcullar gold.'

'So you believe that Carter and McNair were victims of this conspiracy in America?' suggested Hopkins.

Holmes shook his head. 'I did not say so,' he protested. 'I said that they were both murdered by the same party and that the killer's intention was to stop either laying hands on the gold. Therein lies the principal difficulty in this inquiry – in whose interest is the killer or killers acting? We may rule out the United States government, whose man Carter was, and we may rule out the personal interest of the Inverness lawyer. Beyond that there are numerous possibilities of persons acting alone or in concert for personal gain or factious interest. Like the late Thomas Chater.'

'It is, of course, Chater's death that brings us here,' said McBrain. 'You consider that to be connected with the London murders?'

'Indubitably,' replied Holmes. 'I have never been a believer in coincidence. I know that Chater tried to kill me on the first day I was here. I cannot be certain as to his reason, but I imagine that my sudden appearance on the scene had startled him and he took precipitate action. One of the disadvantages of Watson's popularity as a writer is that I must go heavily disguised if I am not to be recognized in almost any circle, and I am sure that my identity was soon no secret in this village.'

'And you believe that Chater was mixed up in the search for the gold?' said Hopkins.

'Certainly,' said Holmes. 'He was an American by birth, an adventurer by trade, one who had chanced his arm in the Yukon looking for gold. How much better to track down a source of gold in Scotland without having to compete with the hordes of the Alaskan goldfields? Why else did such a man choose to settle in one of the most remote parts of Scotland? Whether he came here as an agent of the American conspiracy or as a personal treasure hunter, we cannot know at present, but he was certainly looking for the gold.'

'How would he have heard of the Strathcullar gold?' asked McBrain.

'From those who sent him, if he came as an agent of the conspiracy. Otherwise he may well have picked up the story from his partner Red Ewan Breck in a tale told during some long Alaskan night.'

'And he was killed, almost immediately after his attempt on you,' remarked Hopkins.

Holmes nodded. 'Almost certainly by the same murderer who disposed of Carter and McNair.'

'And have you any inkling as to who that was?' asked the Scotland Yarder.

'I am always unwilling,' said Holmes, 'to theorize far ahead of the available data, and in this case suspicions multiply and data is scarce. Nevertheless, if I had Watson's gambling habit I might venture a shilling or two on the Irishman, Seamus Fisher.'

'And who is he?' asked McBrain.

'Fisher,' said Holmes, 'is a former seaman,

an erstwhile shipmate of the late Chater. When the new road was built across the pass into Strathcullar, Fisher was a ganger on the job and lived in the village for some time. Subsequently he returned and set up home here because, he says, he likes the place and his old friend Chater was here.'

'You do not believe him?' said Hopkins.

'I do not,' said Holmes. 'Coincidences should be treated like rotten fish – dealt with cautiously and destroyed if possible. The coming together of Chater and Fisher in this village is beyond coincidence. Whether together or not, they were treasure hunting.'

'But why would Fisher kill Chater?' pressed McBrain.

'For the same reason that he killed Carter and McNair: to preserve the gold for himself or those for whom he acted. He may well have feared that Chater's attempt on me might lead to an arrest and to Chater talking, thereby drawing attention to Fisher's activities.'

'Is there any other reason to suspect him?' asked Hopkins.

'His accent and his politics,' said Holmes. 'Though he hails from the south of Ireland, he has sailed about the world, he has worked in America and in Scotland and his accent is sufficiently fluid for him to pass as a Highlander, at least in a brief conversation with the maid of the Braemar Hotel. If you recall, Watson, she said that at first she thought McNair's visitor was Irish. In addition, he bears an unusual tattoo, which both Watson and I have seen. It portrays a dagger, dripping blood, over the motto *"Sic Semper Tyrannis"* – not an Irish slogan, not a Fenian motto, but the very words attributed to the alleged murderer of President Lincoln.'

The two policemen sat thoughtfully silent for a moment, then Hopkins reached inside his coat.

'You have complained of lack of fresh data,' he said. 'When we searched McNair's office we found these, slid under the blotter on his desk. Perhaps they will help,' and he passed some sheets of manuscript to Holmes.

McNair's Clue

Holmes' ability to absorb written or printed matter was phenomenal, and it took him little time to read the sheets which had come from the lawyer's blotter.

When he looked up from the papers he began, 'Have you...?' but for once Hopkins forestalled him.

'We have brushed those sheets and the blotter sheets with cigarette ash, as you recommend, Mr Holmes, but all that we discovered was jottings of train times connected with his journey to London.'

Holmes nodded approvingly. 'Well done,' he said.

'Why did he go to London to transact his business with Carter?' I asked.

Holmes looked up at me. 'I imagine that he did not wish to give the American clues as to his identity, nor prematurely reveal the location of the gold,' he said.

He riffled a hand through the pages that he held. 'These,' he said, 'appear to be a set of notes that McNair made as he researched the possible location of the gold. I take it that they are in his hand?'

'Oh, aye,' said McBrain. 'There's nae doubt that's McNair's own fist.'

'Good,' said Holmes, and began to read from the first page.

'"June 1775, a revenue cutter observes what appears to be a Dutch vessel loading cargo on to the beach at Dunfrory, a small east coast port. The cutter gives chase as the Dutchman stands off, but loses his quarry in heavy weather. Returning to the landing site, the revenuers can see that a heavy load has been taken from the beach by pack-horses."'

'Evidently,' commented Holmes, 'they will have believed that they had witnessed a routine delivery by smugglers, but a few days later comes fresh information.' He read the next note.

'"Information from an approver—"'

'What is an approver?' I asked.

'It's what you would call in England an informer, or a crown witness,' explained McBrain.

'Sorry, Holmes,' I said, 'please continue.'

'"Information from an approver,"' Holmes continued, '"that the Dutchman's cargo was gold from France bound for the American rebels, to be shipped from west coast."'

'That'll have put the cat among the

pigeons,' remarked McBrain.

'Oh, it did,' said Holmes, and read on. '"Garrisons at Fort William and Inverness alerted, Royal Navy ships brought to west coast with Revenue sloops to assist." Then the ink changes as though McNair has noted matter from a different source.'

He continued reading. '"Fast patrols sent out from Inverness on most likely route to intercept packtrain, without success. Burgoyne and five hundred infantry move west, scanning any trail, questioning locals, but no sign of the train."'

'Is that the same Burgoyne – "Gentlemanly Johnny" – who surrendered to the Americans at Saratoga?' I asked.

'It almost certainly is,' said Holmes. 'I should be grateful if you would not interrupt unnecessarily, Watson.'

'I was merely about to observe that he didn't seem to have much luck at home or abroad.'

He glanced at me impatiently and continued.

'"Burgoyne believed that the transport of the gold across Scotland would be in Jacobite hands, and concentrated his efforts in areas known to be strongholds of the Stuart cause. These were well known and closely observed at the time – only thirty years after Culloden – and a great deal of searching was carried out in such areas. Scattering bribes to Highlanders loyal to the crown brought in a trickle of information: that the packtrain had passed towards Strathcullar, but was not reported west of the valley. Burgoyne decided that, Strathcullar being a particular centre of Jacobitsm, the gold had been hidden somewhere in that vicinity. He brought the main part of his men to Strathcullar and camped on the northern side of the loch for several weeks. As well as attempting – unsuccessfully – to seduce villagers as approvers, he had the hills, caves, crags and so on searched in detail and the loch dragged from end to end."

'The ink changes again,' remarked Holmes. '"The Royal Navy and Revenuers reported that any vessel from the west coast that might have carried the gold had been stopped and searched, but nothing had been found. At last both Army and Navy agreed that further search was pointless. The coastal patrols were reduced and Burgoyne and his men recalled to Inverness and Fort William, though a spy was left in Strathcullar in case the departure of Burgoyne's searchers encouraged someone to attempt a recovery of the gold. So far as is known that did not occur. All the spy reported was the sudden departure of Mungo Breck for Canada."'

He stopped. 'So far,' he said, 'McNair seems to have been summarizing official documents. Then he becomes more fragmentary, in what seem to be jottings relating to his own researches.'

He resumed reading the notes aloud. '"B's men searched whole area and dragged loch. Did they search the crannogs?"'

'It would have served no purpose,' he commented. 'We know now that the village boys swim from and around the crannogs in summer, looking for traces of the original occupiers. If the gold was concealed on one of those artificial islands, it would have come to light by now.'

He read on. '"Crannogs frequently used by hunters after waterfowl, besides Chater has looked carefully. B proposed blowing up the graveyard on Inish Beg, but the villagers turned very nasty about the proposal and the then laird made representations to B's commander, so it was left alone."'

'"C and I" – presumably that refers to Chater – "have now walked every inch of the valley and seen nothing. We have even looked into adjacent valleys, but they are extremely unlikely. The reason for concealing the gold would have been that they did not believe they could reach the west coast before B caught them. They would need to act swiftly – not risk wasting time by taking a heavily-loaded packtrain up the mountains."

'Then,' said Holmes, 'his notes become even more scrappy.' He read, '"Must be in Strathcullar. Not in loch. Not in river. Not in immediate vicinity if C and I correct. Would never have been in castle."'

'Why not?' I queried.

'Because, Watson, the homes of Jacobite sympathizers were always likely to be raided and searched.'

'And why not in the river or the loch?' asked Hopkins.

'Because,' said my friend, 'Burgoyne's men had searched thoroughly and found nothing, and McNair and Chater had searched themselves with the same result. McNair seems to be summarizing his thoughts here. He notes his attempts and Chater's to obtain information from the villagers, but says that they seemed not to have any tradition of consequence. Then there is a final scribbled note – "Chater's clue. 718".'

He looked up at the two police officers. 'Do you have any idea what that number means?'

They both shook their heads. 'None whatever, Mr Holmes,' admitted McBrain. 'Mr Hopkins and I have puzzled long and hard over that, sir. We looked hard for anything else, but those notes were all that we found.'

Holmes eyed the papers again. 'McNair placed a question mark after the number. Does that, I wonder, mean that he was unsure of the number, or that he was unsure of its value as a clue? Like much more in this matter we cannot be certain, so we must put it aside until we can decipher it.'

'It may be a length,' I hazarded.

'Indeed, Watson,' said Holmes, 'and measured where? And in what? Feet, inches, yards, ells, metres? At present this apparent clue presents a danger – it may divert our attention from other matters. We must put it aside until fresh data confirms or contradicts it. If it is confirmed, then we must consider its meaning.'

'And what will you do in the meantime?' asked McBrain.

'There are certain observations which Watson and I must make, after which I may have to make a brief journey.'

This was news to me. 'I thought,' I said, 'that you had determined to act as bait to draw out our villain?'

'So I had,' Holmes agreed, 'but that was before the arrival of the official police. The presence of these two gentlemen in the village will distract the perpetrator from my absence, I feel sure. I believe you are staying at the Strathcullar Inn? Well, I suggest you make yourselves fully familiar with its denizens, not least Red Ewan Breck and Seamus Fisher. I suggest also that you behave with extreme care. Do not forget that we are seeking a man who has an alarming talent with a knife.'

We took our farewells of the officers and I turned to Holmes.

'What are these observations which we must make?' I enquired.

'I told you earlier,' he said, 'I must make some observations upon the movements of the sun. You were pleased to be flippant about my explanation, but it is true.'

'I'm sorry,' I said, 'but I had thought the sun's movements were adequately observed. It rises in the east and sets in the west and so on.'

'You have accused me,' he said, 'of having no knowledge of astronomy, Watson, but even I know that only on two days in a year does the sun rise in the east and set in the west. Therein lies the problem which I propose to solve. Now, I suggest that we turn in. We shall do some walking tomorrow.'

We had completed our toilet and were lying in our beds, smoking a final pipe. I was about to extinguish the candle when a shot sounded from close by.

'Holmes!' I exclaimed. 'That was a shot!'

'So it was,' he remarked, unperturbed.

I listened for a moment. 'Do you think it may have been a huntsman?' I asked.

'Having regard to the fact that it is the wrong time of year, that it is pitch dark outside, that it was a pistol – not a rifle – shot and that it came from somewhere close to us but behind the cottages, I think not.'

'Then why has someone fired a pistol in the village at this time of night?' I persisted.

'I do not know and will not surmise whether someone has shot themselves, a neighbour's cat or another participant in the gold conspiracy, Watson. What I am certain of is that it is pitch dark and any venture we might make at present to discover the facts would be the height of folly. Goodnight, Watson.'

Saying which he leaned across and extinguished our candle.

I lay awake for some time, trying to find explanations for that pistol shot. When, at last, I fell asleep, my dreams were haunted by the number 718.

Holmes Observations

In my years of association with Sherlock Holmes I have frequently found myself completed baffled by the direction which my friend's thoughts and actions seemed to be taking. I have never been more so than on the next day in Strathcullar.

No sooner had we finished breakfast than Holmes had us out of the house, striding away along the lochside. Each of us bore a knapsack which, in my case, contained the day's provisions supplied by Mrs Mackintosh.

We walked first in a westerly direction, following the loch's shore until we reached its western extremity where it drained into the river again. If Holmes was seeking something it did not appear to me. He seemed to be entirely involved in reaching the end of the loch, and took little if any notice of our path.

It was a fine day and our walk alongside the loch would normally have been a refreshing exercise to me, but Holmes had set a cracking pace from the beginning and grumbled at me occasionally for failing to keep up with him, so that our expedition was not as pleasant to me as it might have been.

When we had rounded the western limit of the loch and were approaching the junction of the lake with its tributary river, we found ourselves picking our way through swampy mosses, where the overflow of the river evidently leaked into the soil. Here the brush grew more thickly as well, so that we had to watch our footsteps carefully and probe ahead of us with our sticks.

We came at last to a more or less dry section of the loch's shore, beside which the river ran and on which sprung a thick coppice of young trees. Here my friend paused and produced from his knapsack a map.

I looked at the swamp through which we had made our way.

'Do you think,' I said, 'that the gold might have been concealed in that morass?'

Holmes looked up from his chart with an expression of annoyance. 'I sincerely hope not, Watson. There are, I suspect, areas of that swamp that are very deep indeed and, while it might prove very easy to drop a considerable weight of gold into them, one can only be appalled at the difficulties of recovering it. If it has, indeed, been concealed therein, it may have to stay there until a new Ice Age scours this valley.'

Suitably reproved I applied myself to looking about the landscape. Holmes continued to examine his map.

'What, exactly, are we seeking here?' I asked, after a while.

'According to the map,' said Holmes, 'there should be an ancient standing stone in this vicinity, on the south bank of the river close to where it issues from the loch. I see no sign of it and can only conclude that it must be hidden by the undergrowth here.'

He took up his stick and advanced on the thicket, probing among the branches, while I moved alongside him doing the same. We had not forced our way far into the copse when we both saw at once a tumble of stones overgrown with moss and almost invisible against the young greenery about them.

We pushed through to the cairn and Holmes knelt beside the stones. 'I am right,' he said. 'These are the remains of a Pictish marker stone of some kind. Look, Watson!'

He scraped his pocketknife along the mossy side of one stone and the scrape revealed the outline of one of those fantastic beasts with which the Picts decorated their stones.

I had been squatting against a larger fragment of stone. 'But this,' I said, rapping my stick upon it, 'appears to be a cross.'

He came across and together we raised the piece of stone until we could see all of its shape.

'A Celtic cross!' I exclaimed, for it was clearly the well-known wheeled cross of the Celts.

'And very crudely carved,' remarked my friend. 'Nowhere near as good as the animal carvings on the other stones.'

'What do you make of it?' I asked.

'I have seen similar practises in Brittany,' he said. 'Devout Christians find these prehistoric relics of paganism offensive, so they attempt to destroy the original significance by carving the top of the stone into a cross.'

'But here someone seems to have done that, then someone else has come along and smashed the whole thing. Was that because it had a cross on it?' I asked.

Holmes shook his head. 'The Highlanders are usually very devout. I cannot see them smashing a pillar that had been carved with a cross. I confess, the whole thing is singular and puzzling, but it is not my most immediate concern.'

He pressed into the scrub, pushing towards the loch's shore and occasionally using his pocketknife to trim away a branch or two from a sapling. When he had finished I realized that it was now just possible to see through the greenery and across the loch.

Holmes took his field glasses, a notebook and a compass from his knapsack. He glanced at me, where I stood wondering if I had any useful part to play in his efforts.

'I shall be a little while in making my observations,' he said. 'You might like to use the time to refresh yourself, as we shall be moving on when I have done here.'

Still in complete bewilderment, I settled myself on a piece of the fallen stone and explored my knapsack. As I ate Holmes busied himself with careful sightings, measurements and jottings in his notebook. When he seemed to have exhausted the possibilities of the compass and field glasses, he drew from his knapsack a curious wooden device of more or less triangular form and began to make a new range of sightings with it.

After about half an hour he packed away his instruments and cut a long slender stick from a sapling, trimming away its twigs. Tying his handkerchief to the top of this wand, he thrust the other end into the earth just in front of the heap of stones, then stepped back with an expression of satisfaction.

'That,' he remarked, 'should be visible

with the glasses from the eastern pass.'

I had been about to suggest that he too might take his luncheon, but it occurred to me that he was in that mood where the urgent pursuit of a line of thought brushed away all thoughts of sustenance. He drew his watch from his pocket, glanced at it and commanded me, 'Come, Watson. It is a fair step from here to the shoulder of the pass.'

Stuffing the remains of my meal into the knapsack I rose and followed him as he pushed his way out of the brush. As we stepped out into the daylight I caught a quick flash of sunlight reflected from glass on the rough slope behind the village, as I had done when we had visited Inish Beg.

'Holmes,' I exclaimed, 'we are being observed again!' And I pointed with my stick.

He glanced in the direction that I indicated.

'So we are,' he said. 'I am glad to see that our opponent takes such an interest in our efforts.'

We made our way carefully across the small swamp and took the road eastwards. Soon Holmes was setting a cracking pace along the road, through the village and up towards the eastern pass. By the time we reached the Pictish pillar I was sweating profusely and glad of the opportunity to sprawl on the grass at the roadside while my friend went about his arcane operations.

Once again the field glasses, compass and notebook were deployed, and it became evident to me at one point that he was taking a bearing from the stone beside us to the handkerchief flag which he had left at the far end of the loch. From time to time he consulted his watch and noted the time, while he sighted at the sun with his triangular instrument.

Holmes had, seemingly, forgotten my existence, so I took the opportunity to continue my interrupted luncheon. Soon the warm air, the scent of heather and my full stomach put me into a doze and I lay at length upon the grass.

By the time I awoke it was late afternoon and Holmes, his exercises seemingly complete, sat on the grass nearby, smoking and looking over the landscape.

'Holmes,' I said, 'if we were taking a walking holiday in reality we could not wish for better than this,' indicating with my arm the glorious landscape that lay below us.

He took his pipe from his mouth and smiled, a trifle sardonically I thought. 'I am sure you are right, Watson, but we must remember our purposes – to trap a killer and to locate a hoard of gold. Now, if you will allow me a few minutes to make one final observation, we can make our way homewards.'

He took out his little boxwood instrument and pointed towards the sun, after checking the time by his watch, noting the result of whatever measurement he had made into his notebook.

Once he had packed away his devices he swung up from the grass.

'Come, Watson,' he said. 'Now, when we have fed, I must try to make sense of all this.'

Our homeward road had at least the virtue of being a downhill one and Holmes did not now seem in such a hurry, so that I surmised his measurements, whatever they were, had proved successful.

Soon we were at Mrs Mackintosh's tea table with the now customary spread before us. Once the table was cleared, Holmes produced a large-scale map of Strathcullar and pored over it, frequently consulting his notebook while he began the construction of a chart on a large sheet of plain paper. I could not understand his operations and was sure that any assistance which I volunteered would have been unwelcome, so I passed the evening with a book.

Mrs Mackintosh had waited some time to serve our supper before Holmes put up his papers and instruments.

'I take it that whatever measurements you

have been taking have been successful?' I enquired as we drank a cup of tea.

'That they are as accurate as circumstances permit, I am sure,' he replied. 'Whether they are accurate enough for our purposes will have to be the opinion of another.'

'Will they lead to the gold?' I asked.

He shook his head. 'I doubt if they will do so directly, but I hope that they may confirm a suspicion that I have. To do that I shall have to go away for a few days.'

'Go away!' I exclaimed. 'Where are we going?'

'You, Watson, may remain in Strathcullar. I would not like our quarry to feel that I have lost interest in him. I must go to Edinburgh, where I should be able to find an astronomer who can assist me in certain calculations from my observations.'

'And what do you wish me to do in Strathcullar?' I requested.

'I shall be grateful if you will make yourself seen about the village, frequent the inn, keep a discreet eye upon the Irishman and, if possible, try to ensure that nobody else gets killed.'

A Visit from the Doctor

It was the afternoon of the following day when I had a visitor. Holmes had departed for the railway station after luncheon. I was considering taking a constitutional about the village when Mrs Mackintosh informed me that Dr Guthrie was at the door for me.

I was aware that Dr Guthrie was the local practitioner for whom I had substituted when Chater was killed, and I hoped that his arrival did not indicate another fatality. I asked our landlady to bring a fresh pot of tea and show the doctor in.

Guthrie, when he joined me, turned out to be a short, plump individual, round-faced and pink-complexioned under a thick head of silver hair. He wore small, gold-rimmed eyeglasses and, despite the warm day, a suit of thick, pale grey tweed. We shook hands and I offered him a chair and a cup of tea.

He dropped his medical bag beside the hearth and sat down.

'I'm sorry, Doctor, that I was not here to pay a social call when you first arrived in

Strathcullar,' he began, 'but I was up the next valley dealing with an outbreak of measles. We live an extremely healthy existence here, but now and then disease finds us out and plays havoc in these little valley villages. It has to be stamped out before it is carried to a neighbouring village. Well, I think I have done that with the measles, and while I was doing it you had to stand in on a murder.'

I nodded. 'It was little enough,' I said. 'The poor fellow was stone dead when I saw him and had been very finally and effectually stabbed.'

'So I heard,' he said, 'but I was surprised. The folk of Strathcullar are not saints and sometimes settle their differences violently, but they do not usually do so with a knife. The local weapons of choice are fisticuffs or a blunt instrument, with occasionally a fire-arm in the hunting season. A knife suggests an outsider.'

'Holmes said much the same,' I said.

'Ah, yes, your celebrated colleague. Is he here at present? Someone said that he had gone away.'

'His inquiries have taken a particular direction,' I said, 'and he has had to go to Edinburgh for a few days to pursue them. Was it Holmes that you wished to see?'

He shook his head. 'No, no, Doctor. It is

not a detective but a doctor that I need. I would like, if you will permit me, to trespass upon your time again and ask you for a second opinion.'

'Ask away,' I invited. 'There is no trespass. With Holmes away there is little for me to do. What seems to be your problem?'

Guthrie frowned. 'I wish I knew, Doctor.' He shook his head and began again.

'I have told you that I fear the spread of disease in the area. We are remote from help, a long way from the railway and further from a good hospital. To ship a seriously ill or injured patient into town would be a nightmare, even since the road was improved. At many times in the winter when the snow is deep, it would be totally impossible. With these things in mind, I have always striven to identify and stifle any infectious condition as soon as it appears in Strathcullar and taken measures to prevent it spreading. I am all too well aware that a sudden outbreak could wipe out the entire village.'

I nodded and he continued.

'I do not pretend to a wide medical expertise, but I have practised here for more than twenty years without noticeably bad results, and I have managed to deal with those medical situations which have arisen. Now, however, I find myself faced with a situation that baffles me. For that reason I trust you will bring your experience to the aid of a colleague.'

'Well,' I said, 'I am, of course, entirely at your service, Doctor, but I must warn you that I have not practised medicine, except in emergencies, for some twenty years.'

'I am aware of that,' he said, 'but you were formerly a general practitioner in a big city and you have served with the Army abroad. Your experience is bound to be wider than mine.'

'Is there nobody else you can consult?' I asked.

He shook his head.

'I have wired a description of the symptoms to Inverness, but they have made no helpful suggestions, other than to remark that it sounds like some kind of digestive condition and could be some form of poisoning.'

'Poisoning!' I exclaimed, and there came into my mind Holmes' sardonic warning about not permitting any more deaths. Surely our killer had not now taken to poison!

'Of course I will come at once,' I said. 'Where is your patient?'

'At the castle,' said Guthrie. 'It is the laird.'

'Great Heavens!' I said. 'Let me fetch my bag.'

In a minute I had my bag and we stood outside on the jetty, waiting for Lacky to return from the island.

A solemn-faced Ewan Breck answered the door of the castle to us.

'Dr Guthrie! And you've brought Dr Watson!' he exclaimed. 'I'll show you up right away, gentlemen. Please follow me.'

The old retainer led us up two flights of stairs to a chamber at the front of the building, where the laird lay in an old-fashioned four-poster bed propped on a pile of pillows and a bolster. A young housemaid was attending him.

'Come in, gentlemen, come in!' he welcomed us, though it was immediately evident that his voice was weak and uncertain.

'I have taken the liberty,' said Guthrie, 'of asking my colleague Dr Watson to consult with me.'

'That is no problem, none at all,' said the laird. 'I would welcome any useful observations which the good doctor may make.'

I stepped forward to the bedside and viewed the patient's appearance carefully. He was certainly not the robustly cheerful man in early middle age with whom I had dined days ago. Now his facial colour had fled, being replaced by a sickly, yellowish pallor. Large dark shadows hung under his eyes, which were clouded and weeping.

I took his pulse and applied my stethoscope to his chest. The pulse was feeble and irregular and his breathing was weak and laboured. I was soon sure that his condition was a serious one.

'When did this begin?' I asked.

'Yesterday morning,' he replied. 'I had eaten well and heartily the night before, but I awoke in the morning feeling sick and listless. When I tried to rise I almost fell, I was so weak.'

'And what had you eaten on the previous evening?'

'I had dined on a large portion of haggis with vegetables, all prepared by Mrs Herd.'

'That,' I said, 'should not have made you unwell. A haggis, properly prepared and cooked, should do you good, rather than harm. As to Mrs Herd's cookery, from what we enjoyed the other night she is evidently an excellent cook. Are you able to eat anything now? Have you eaten since?'

'Very little,' he said. 'I cannot take any solid food. It will not stay down. Mrs Herd has been sending up a good broth for me and I have managed a little of that.'

He gestured feebly towards a chest of drawers, atop which stood a basin covered with a napkin. I stepped across and lifted the cloth. The basin was half-full of a rich brown broth and one sniff told me that it had not gone sour in any way. On the contrary; it smelled of meat and vegetables and should, in my opinion, have done nothing but good in building up the strength of an invalid.

I turned back to the bed and reflected on the large handkerchief that was bound about the laird's head.

'The broth should do you no harm,' I said. 'Quite the opposite. Tell me, are you suffering any pains in the head?'

'Not specifically,' said the patient. 'I am weak and feel dizzy much of the time. My eyes won't focus for very long. The turban arrangement is because my hair seems to be coming out.'

'Your hair is falling out!' I exclaimed. I had been able to make nothing specific of his other symptoms, but his falling hair struck me as a sinister manifestation.

I offered the laird some general good advice and drew Guthrie from the chamber. Outside we conferred in a low tone.

'You see,' he said, 'why I can make nothing of it? Last week he was a healthy, active man, who has never suffered other than minor ailments. Now he presents the appearance of someone who is slipping away, yet I can detect no symptoms of any disease as such. It is more as if his body was failing and he was dying prematurely of old age.'

I nodded. 'I certainly believe that his condition is extremely grave. His lungs and circulation are both feeble, and either might fail at any time. Like you, I see no trace of disease as such, but the hair loss concerns me gravely.'

'What do you think it means?'

'When we dined with him the other night he was a robust man in early middle age, whose hair had not lost its colour and appeared luxuriant. Now he is enfeebled, with weak lungs and circulation and his hair is falling out.'

'What do you suggest?' asked Guthrie.

'That you give him tonics and stimulate his heart and lungs in any way that you can; that you keep an extremely careful eye on anything he eats or drinks.'

'Dr Watson!' Guthrie exclaimed. 'What are you suggesting?'

'You called me in, Guthrie, because I have had experience which you lack. One of those experiences has been years of association with a major authority on poisons. I have very little doubt that the laird is being poisoned.'

An American Stranger

I had intended to make a visit to the inn on that evening, but the laird's condition and the burden imposed upon me by Sherlock Holmes made me restless. I passed the afternoon with a book, but could not settle to my reading.

I found myself constantly running over the laird's symptoms in my mind, striving to find, in some corner of my memory, any recollection of something seen or read that might lead me to a proper diagnosis of his condition. Again and again my thoughts turned to poisoning, and I wished heartily that Sherlock Holmes, with his encyclopaedic knowledge of poisons, would be back soon.

The thought of my friend's absence turned my mind in another direction and made me reflect on the situation in which he had left me. Both Holmes and I had warned each other of the dangers of Strathcullar but it was not that which concerned me; if I do not court danger so far as Holmes sometimes appears to, I believe at the least that I am as steady as the next man in facing it when it arises. What concerned me was the feeling that I might fail in Holmes' expectations of me. On a number of occasions Sherlock Holmes has left me to hold the fort, to appear in his stead or to pursue an inquiry on his behalf. I do not believe that he has ever been satisfied with my efforts and, in some cases, has been overtly sarcastic about my attempts. It was not the thought of his sardonic tongue that worried me – after twenty years I have learned to suffer that – but the consideration that he might have occasion to berate me in this matter because I had failed in the one respect on which he had instructed me directly and allowed somebody else to be murdered.

With these gloomy thoughts in mind I put aside my book and began to review the entire case in my mind, insofar as I understood it. I knew nothing of the purposes of Holmes' measurements, nor the reason for his visit to Edinburgh, but I thought that I understood the history of the case reasonably. I turned over the whole chain of occurrences in my head, considering each one carefully along with any conclusions or inferences which Holmes had drawn, while considering whether I would make the same deduction.

It was in this process that I recollected the pistol shot which we had heard as we went to bed. Whilst I had fully accepted my friend's reasons for not investigating the matter immediately, I was less than sure of his suggestions that somebody in Strathcullar was firing at a stray cat. I noted that we had never pursued the matter and determined to do so.

Having hit on this idea I felt a small degree less helpless and undirected. I made a hearty tea and, in the early part of a splendid summer evening, set out to visit the Strathcullar Inn and commence my enquiries.

After leaving our lodgings I stood for a few minutes, smoking a cigarette and admiring the beauty of the loch in the evening sunlight. I had finished my cigarette and was about to continue on my way to the inn when a voice called from my right.

Looking round I saw a man striding down the lower slope of the eastern pass to where the road ran levelly into the village. I stood and watched his approach, surprised at seeing a pedestrian making his way down from the pass. I could only imagine that he was one of those enthusiasts who walk long distances in the Highlands and that he was making for the village before nightfall.

As he drew nearer his appearance seemed

to confirm my belief. He was an oldish man with silvering dark hair and a weather-beaten complexion above a greying beard and moustache. He wore blue-tinted spectacles and carried a fairly considerable bundle slung at his back, while his right hand wielded a tall ash staff.

'Well,' he exclaimed, dropping himself on to a bench beside the jetty, 'that's a relief! I wasn't at all sure I'd get here by sundown, but here I am and I see the Strathcullar Inn just over there. I hope they'll have a bed for a weary traveller.'

'I cannot say,' I replied. 'They certainly let beds, but we are in the holiday season.'

'Well,' he said again, 'I surely hope they have one tonight.'

'You have come far?' I asked. 'All the way across the hills from the railway station?'

He nodded. 'Yes, indeed, all the way from the railhead.'

I had noted from the start that his accent was American, which, in the circumstances, put me on the alert.

'You are an American?' I said.

He smiled and held out a long brown hand. 'Yes, sir. Phineas G. Macleod at your service, sometime doctor of music at the Boston Conservatoire. And whom do I have the honour of addressing?'

I shook the proffered hand. 'Another

doctor,' I replied, 'though of the medical variety. I am John Watson.'

'Are you the doctor to this lovely village? You're not a Scotchman,' he said.

'No, no,' I said. 'I'm a Londoner nowadays. I'm merely here on a walking tour with a friend, but he's had to go to Edinburgh on business. You look tired. Let me prescribe a glass of beer and a nip of the local malt whisky.'

He stood up and we moved towards the inn. On the way he explained that he was retired from teaching and now went about studying the musical productions of the peasantry in remote places.

'My ancestry is partly from Scotland,' he said, 'as my name must have told you, so I am spending this summer here, hearing their music and songs and listening to their tales.'

When we arrived at the inn, I introduced him to mine host, who was pleased to offer him a room. While he went to the room I took a drink with Hopkins and McBrain, who were seated together in a corner of the front bar.

'Are you making any progress?' I enquired as I sat down.

Both of them shook their heads.

'The people of this village,' said McBrain, 'are the most affable and welcoming I have ever encountered, they will chatter to us about anything in the world, apart from the fact that there is a murderer amongst them.' He snorted and reapplied himself to his drink.

Across the bar I could see the two Americans who were lodging in the village. 'What about them?' I asked Hopkins, quietly, while I nodded discreetly towards the foreigners.

'They are what they seem, so far as we can tell. I've had the Yard check them out with the American police. They wired us to say that those two blokes match the descriptions of the names they're using. Apparently they're businessmen who had some reason to be in London earlier and then moved up here to do a bit of walking. There is one thing, though.'

'What's that?' I asked.

'Both of them were in London at the date of the murders of Carter and McNair.'

'Were they?' I said thoughtfully. 'Do you think they might have done it?'

'Not really,' said Hopkins. 'Neither of them limp, both of them are too short, and I doubt if either of them could throw a skean-dhu as accurately as our man.'

I nodded. 'So we really aren't any further forward,' I said, 'unless Holmes brings back what he calls "fresh data" from Inverness.' I thought about my earlier reflections. 'Tell me,' I said, 'did either of you hear a shot late the other night? A pistol shot, from somewhere at the back here, behind the cottages.'

McBrain chuckled. 'Aye,' he said, 'we heard it, so we made enquiries about it the next morning. That's one thing we solved completely. We know the name of the victim and where he's buried.'

I looked at them, nonplussed. 'Surely Holmes wasn't right again? He said it might be somebody taking a potshot at a stray cat.'

They both laughed.

'Near enough for a guess,' said McBrain. 'The fact is that auld Jock, Ewan Breck's auld dog, was very poorly. The years ganged up on him and he needed to be put down, but Breck couldnae dae it. So he asked the Irishman to do the honours, which is what we heard.'

'We learned one thing, though,' said Hopkins. 'Seamus Fisher seems to be in possession of Tam Chater's revolver.'

'I don't know that it helps at all,' I said. 'It's his skills with knives we need to know about.'

'More to the point than dead dogs,' said McBrain, 'we hear that the laird's been taken ill and that you've been to see him. Is there anything in that we should look into?'

'I don't know,' I said, truthfully. I proceeded to give them a summary of the situation, ending with my opinion.

'Poisoned!' they both said, simultaneously.

'How do you think it's been done and why?' asked Hopkins.

'I wish I was sure,' I said. 'I can only say that it's my opinion that he's suffering from some kind of poisoning, but if he is I can't say how it was administered. All his food is cooked by Mrs Herd, who's a very good cook, so he's unlikely to have been accidentally poisoned by bad meat or fish or anything like that.'

'So, it's got to be deliberate,' said Hopkins.

'If, indeed, he's been poisoned, then I cannot see it being accidental.'

'Then who is at the castle to drop a little something in his soup?' said McBrain.

'I'm not sure,' I said. 'Ewan Breck stays there, and Mrs Herd, and there's a parlour-maid. Breck seems to be entirely and devotedly loyal to the laird. If Mrs Herd wanted to poison him, she might do so at any time. It seems foolhardy, to say the least, to do it when there are two private detectives and two official police in the village.'

They nodded, but Hopkins said, 'That leaves the parlourmaid.'

We both looked at him in astonishment.

'Well,' he said, 'she might be doing it for somebody else.'

McBrain snorted. 'That kind of thing may

happen all the time in London, but it doesnae happen in the Highlands.'

Hopkins turned his lip down and addressed himself to his glass.

'Since we first came here people keep telling us that nobody's been murdered here for a century or more, but Tam Chater was.'

A firm hand fell on my shoulder and an American voice said, 'Who was murdered here? I thought these Highland villages had been havens of peace since the Jacobite Rebellions?'

I turned to find Macleod standing behind me. Quickly I introduced him to the two officers, explaining that a recent murder had brought them here, but adding no details. Then I drew him away to the bar and bought drinks, taking him through to the rear parlour afterwards.

Seamus Fisher and Ewan Breck were there in their customary seats. I bought them whisky and introduced Macleod. Breck's old eyes lit up at the mention of Macleod's quest for ancient Scots songs and melodies.

'I used to be no end of a fiddler,' he said, 'before my hands began to go, but I've still got a head full of the airs and the words of a good many songs.'

Macleod rubbed his hands with expectation and drew out a notebook. Soon he and

Breck were deep in discourse over folk melodies. I took the opportunity to engage Fisher in conversation, but he was as slippery as an eel. With perfect politeness and many an Irish pleasantry he replied to my questions with answers that were minimal in their information. By closing time I had learned little that I had not known before; that he had taken to the sea as a youth, had gone ashore in America and while there had taken up navvying on the railways. I heard again the story of his arrival in Strathcullar with a road gang and his decision to settle there, plus his great delight when his old seagoing chum Tam Chater had the same idea.

'Did you not think it a remarkable coincidence,' I asked, 'that you and Tam Chater should both fetch up far from your native places, in the same little valley in Scotland?'

Fisher took his pipe from his mouth.

'I believe that you've knocked about the world a bit yourself,' he said. 'Surely you'll have observed that coincidences happen more often than people believe who only stay at home?' And he launched into a complicated tale about three shipwrecks which kept us occupied until the inn closed.

The Phantom of Inish Beg

It was on one of the days of Holmes' absence that, after attending the laird in the morning and lunching in my lodgings, I decided to take the air at the lochside.

I had seated myself on the bench by the jetty when I heard a voice calling, 'Dr Watson! Dr Watson!'

Looking about me I saw no one immediately, but I recognized the voice as that of young Lacky, and so strolled along the jetty to see if he was in his boat below. As I reached the farther end he appeared on the steps.

'Dr Watson,' he said, 'I saw you on your own and wanted a word. I couldnae very well say it in front of Dr Guthrie this morning...'

'Why? What's your problem, Lacky?' If I had been asked, I would have laid money on the proposition that the youth was troubled by one of those matters that commonly bother growing lads, and that he was too embarrassed to speak to the village doctor about it.

An expression of embarrassment crossed his features, almost confirming my diagnosis, so that I was all the more surprised when he spoke again.

'Doctor,' he said, 'do you believe in bogles?'

'In bogles!' I exclaimed. 'You mean ghosts and spirits and that?'

'Aye,' he agreed. 'Bogles and speerits. Are they real?'

I shook my head forcibly. 'No, Lacky,' I said. 'I know that many people do believe that the dead return, but they are mistaken. A very good friend of mine believes that ghosts exist, but he is wrong. Both Mr Holmes and I are quite sure that what people mistake for ghosts are natural events and occurrences which we do not yet understand.'

He looked down at his boot toes and said, 'So if I saw something I thought was a bogle, I'd be wrong? Is that it?'

'Yes,' I said. 'You may well have seen something, but whatever it may have been it wasn't a ghost. What have you seen, Lacky?'

He glanced around him, then drew a deep breath, as though nerving himself to unburden his mind.

'I've been sleeping in my boat since the laird has been ill. The nights are warm now and I take a blanket and a cushion and lie in the boat. Then, if Mrs Herd needs Doctor Guthrie, she can call across from the castle and I can fetch him the faster.'

I nodded, and silently applauded the boy's sterling sense of loyalty.

'Well,' he went on, 'last night I took Ewan Breck, my great-uncle, back to the castle from the inn and I pulled back here and settled down. I dozed off, and it was about midnight when I woke. I had a funny feeling that something wasnae right, so I speired about.'

He paused. 'That was when I saw a light moving on Inish Beg. Now you know, Doctor, there's naething on that island except dead people, but there was a light moving about there, as sure as I'm standing here.'

He looked at me truculently, as though challenging me to deny his story.

'And you saw and heard no boat?' I said.

He shook his head. 'I admit I was asleep before I saw yon light, but anybody who took one of the boats out from here would have been gey silent, not to wake me.'

I nodded. 'What,' I asked, 'did you do when you saw the light?'

'I was scared, Doctor,' he admitted. 'Once I was absolutely certain that I really had seen a light, I took my blanket and my cushion and I went home for the rest of the night.'

'And you never heard a boat coming back to the village?' I enquired.

'No, Doctor.'

'Well, Lacky, if you saw a light – and I'm sure you did – then there must have been somebody carrying it,' I assured him.

He looked at me doubtfully, and I realized that I was confronting a lifetime of superstition passed down from untold generations. Nevertheless, I had no intention of misleading the boy and I was sure that I knew what Sherlock Holmes would expect of me.

'Lacky,' I said, 'you're a brave lad. If I take a pistol with us, will you row me to Inish Beg tonight?'

His eyes bulged. 'Row you to Inish Beg after dark!' he exclaimed. 'Doctor, I wouldnae dae that for a whole golden guinea!'

I stood my ground and felt in my pocket. 'Then,' I said, 'what about two whole golden guineas?' And I held them out in my hand.

A painful expression crossed the boy's face as he wrestled with this dilemma, but at last cupidity triumphed over superstition.

'Very well,' he said. 'But you make sure you've your pistol and plenty of bullets.'

We agreed to meet an hour before the inn closed, so that we would be well away before anyone was passing along the front of the village. I went home to ponder the meaning of Lacky's story, with little success.

At the appointed hour we took off for the island. It was a dim night with no moonlight, but Lacky assured me that nobody had gone to Inish Beg before us. We landed on the furthermost side and pulled the boat well up on to the little strip of shingle before settling ourselves in the scrubby grass that fringed the cemetery wall. No sooner were we settled than Lacky was importuning me to show him my pistol and bullets, by way of confirming that we were adequately protected.

'Lacky,' I said, 'if you really believe in ghosts and – what did you call them? Bogles? – then you must, surely believe that they have no physical bodies. They cannot be harmed by a bullet if that really is the case.'

'It's all very well for you to have scientific theories, Doctor, but scientific theories won't help you when you've a great gibbering bogle at your heels. Besides, if you have the right of it, and it's only a human being that we have to deal with, it might turn out to be the fellow that stuck a knife into puir Tam Chater, and I'd be happier to have a pistol about then.'

We had been in position for some time

when sounds were borne across the water that told us the inn was closing. It was not very long after that that Lacky nudged me and hissed, 'Listen, Doctor!'

The sound of oars, muffled in their row-locks, could be heard, moving towards us. We lowered our heads, so that anyone land-ing on the nearside of the island would be unaware of us.

Minutes passed while the beat of the muf-fled oars drew closer, then we heard a boat's prow grate on the shingle of the opposite side. Soon footsteps betrayed someone who had come ashore and entered the graveyard by one of the narrow gateways beside the coffin rest.

The scrape of a match told us that the newcomer was lighting a lantern and, be-lieving that his eyes would be confused by the flare of the match, I risked lifting my head above the wall. I could see a tall man kneeling in the centre of the cemetery, adjusting a dark lantern, but the viewpoint and lighting were not such that I could identify him.

When his lantern was set to a narrow beam, he began to examine the gravestones systematically, stooping by each one and peering at it carefully by the lantern's thin slice of light. As he moved about the com-pound, Lacky and I crept noiselessly around the perimeter wall, keeping always at his back. That enabled us to watch over the parapet more readily, without the danger that he would look up and see one or both of us outlined against the water of the loch.

He had covered many of the graves and begun to move in his search towards the little mortuary, when something astonishing occurred. From the inky darkness of the building's doorway came a sound.

It is difficult to describe the noise that issued from the ancient building, save to say that it was some kind of deep, reverberating, pained groan. Lacky and I, who had been in the process of shifting our position, froze, and the intruder turned from the stone he had been examining and slammed shut the slide of his lantern while peering towards the sound.

For several seconds nothing happened. Then a second sound, louder than but similar to the first, rolled from the dark entry of the mortuary. A moment later something glimmered in the gloom of the doorway and I heard the man with the lantern exclaim, 'Saints preserve us!'

Lacky crouched beside me, shivering silently, and I admit that my own nerves had been considerably rattled.

'What is it, Doctor?' the frightened boy whispered.

'Whatever it is,' I answered, 'it is not a ghost or spirit.' I hope I said it with assurance, but I have never been so doubtful of the statement's truth.

I began to slither, as silently as possible, over the low wall into the cemetery, and I account it to Lacky's considerable credit that, terrified as he was, he followed me.

The slight noise of our movement seemed not to have reached the intruder, for he still stood, lantern shut, watching the mortuary doorway as though turned to stone.

From our new position I could see better what it was that glimmered in the inky doorway. There were two luminous shapes, and at first I took them to be some kind of birds or luminous insects. It was only when my eyes became more accustomed to straining across the dark graveyard that I realized what I was seeing – a pair of faintly luminescent human hands were floating in that dark entry, making passes like an orchestral conductor.

I must have been at least as frightened as Lacky, for my mind could conceive of no known phenomena that would produce what I was seeing. At last the spell that bound our intruder lessened, it seemed, for he took one determined step towards the mortuary. Immediately another sound broke forth, and this time the spectral groan seemed to have a distinctly threatening quality.

I forced myself to take a silent step forward and pulled my gun from my pocket. Whatever creature hid in the dark mortuary seemed to be aggressive, and I reasoned that I might soon have to quell that aggression.

Some such thought seems to have stirred the intruder, for he took another firm step forwards.

The pair of hands that floated in the arched doorway flew together. For seconds they fluttered closely and soon I saw that something else was appearing in between them. It was as though the strange hands were plucking something from the surrounding blackness and moulding it into a third object, which they caressed and shaped.

At last the luminous fingers seemed to have completed their task for, after a last sweep, they fell away to each side, revealing that the object between them was a human skull – an eyeless, toothless, grinning death's head, which gleamed with the same greeny-yellowy luminescence.

Suddenly the two hands turned in the air and pointed to the floating skull. The toothless mouth opened and a hoarse, mocking laugh rang across the island.

It was too much for our intruder. With a muttered phrase, which I believe was a prayer, he ran for the wall and leapt it, near to where he had left his boat. In seconds we heard him pulling rapidly away from Inish Beg.

Lacky, though he still stood at my back, was whispering the Lord's Prayer, but paused long enough to hiss, 'Come away, Doctor. I told you there was bogles here!'

Not at all sure that my Adams .450 was capable of inflicting any harm on the creature in the mortuary, I nevertheless kept the weapon pointed. As I watched, first one hand, then the other, passed over the face of the apparition, and soon its luminescence decreased until all three vanished completely into the darkness from which they had sprung.

It crossed my mind to have the boy light a lantern and examine the mortuary, but Lacky was still reciting prayers and tugging at my sleeve. To tell the truth, it was with some relief that I gave way to his urgings to leave the island.

On the way back across the loch both Lacky and I were silent for a long time. We had covered more than two-thirds of the journey to the jetty when the boy spoke at last.

'You said, Doctor,' he spoke accusingly, 'that there is no such thing as a ghost.'

'And you saw,' I said, 'that what carried the light was a man – a live man.'

'Aye, it was,' he conceded, 'but what was it in that hut thing? That wasnae a man, not unless he was a deid man, Doctor.'

'I admit,' I said, 'that I cannot explain what we saw in the entrance to the mortuary, but I can assure you that, whatever it was, it was quite natural.'

'Aye,' said the lad, totally unconvinced, and bent again to his oars.

The Return of Sherlock Holmes

After the bizarre events of that night, I was quite glad that the following days became almost a routine. Each morning I would accompany Dr Guthrie to the castle and examine the laird. He grew not one whit better, day by day. His hair continued to fall out and his appetite became so poor that he could no longer take Mrs Herd's nourishing broth. He was living entirely on cordials and stimulants prescribed by Guthrie. Every day I was prepared for the worst as we rowed across to Inish Mor and I continued to hope that Sherlock Holmes would return, with his expert knowledge of poisons, before the worst happened.

After luncheon at Mrs Mackintosh's I spent the afternoons strolling about the shores of the loch. Once or twice I got young Lacky to take me out on the water on a sunny afternoon, and once I took the opportunity to probe his views on Seamus the ganger.

'I dinnae care for the man, Doctor,' he

said forthrightly. 'Not that he's ever done me any harm that I know about, but he's too smooth in the tongue and too shifty in the eyes for me. I wouldnae be surprised if it wasnae Seamus who went for Mr Holmes that night when we came back from the castle.'

'Really?' I said. 'What makes you say that?'

'People hereabout don't throw knives,' he said, echoing Holmes' view. 'The ghillies carry knives to gralloch deer, and they might use one in a flare-up if it was already aboot them, but they wouldnae know how to throw one. Whoever that was that tried to trap us on the jetty that night could throw one.'

'And what makes you think it was Seamus?' I pressed.

'He lives just along the village from my mother's house. I've seen him from our back window. There's an auld scraggly stump of tree behind his house and I've seen him spend half an afternoon standing in his back garden, throwing a knife at that auld tree. He's good. He can hit what he wants to hit.'

'What sort of knife are we talking about, Lacky?' I enquired.

'I don't know how you might call it. Not a hunting knife like the ghillies use, nor a pocketknife. A sort of dagger, like the one that was thrown at Mr Holmes.'

'You've never seen him throw a skean-dhu?' I asked. 'Have you ever seen anyone throw one?'

He smiled. 'Nay, Doctor, I've never seen him throw a skean-dhu. I've never seen anyone throw one. I doubt you could throw one very far or very true. They're not made for throwing.'

I was pleased to have achieved the small success of establishing that Fisher was an expert with a knife, and now set myself to establishing whether he had the limp which Holmes had reckoned to be a mark of the Regent's Park killer. He was certainly tall enough and strong enough to be our man, and he could pass himself off as a Scot. I had never seen him walk for long enough to determine whether he limped.

I passed a number of evenings at the Strathcullar Inn, always in the back parlour with Breck, Fisher and the American Macleod. The old Scot and the American seemed to have become a twosome, chattering away together, oblivious of Fisher and me. Sometimes their conversation shifted into Gaelic, which Macleod spoke with an American accent, causing Breck a great deal of amusement.

It all seemed very innocent, but I had grown suspicious of the number of Americans who seemed to gravitate to this Highland backwater. Holmes had scorned the idea that the presence of Chater and Fisher was a coincidence and I believed that the Boston music teacher was something other than he seemed. While drinking with Fisher I kept an eye and an ear cocked to observe Ewan Breck and Macleod, and soon observed that, particularly while chatting in Gaelic, Breck kept a wary eye on Fisher.

With Seamus the ganger I got nowhere. His conversation continued to be bland and general, offering little clue to his background or his real thoughts. If I raised American topics, he would respond with either broad reminiscences of unnamed people and places or claim to have no knowledge of American politics.

In between these exercises I turned my mind frequently to 'McNair's clue' – the number 718 – but I made no progress there either. If it was a distance, one would need a starting point and a direction, which we had not got. If it was something else, it was impenetrable.

I returned from one of my morning visits to the laird one day in time to see the carrier's trap setting out for the railway. When I entered my lodgings I was surprised to see Dr Macleod awaiting me in the landlady's parlour.

'Good morning, Doctor,' he said. 'I'm sorry to intrude upon you, but I believe that we have matters to discuss. Not the least being the laird's health.'

'Really?' I said. 'I had thought you were a doctor of music. The laird is presently attended by Dr Guthrie, his regular physician, with myself as a consultant. I fail to see what help you may give.'

'Now, Doctor, I understand that you regard my suggestion that you discuss the laird's health with me as an impertinence, but let me tell you that I was not always a musician. I have some knowledge of poisons.'

'Poisons!' I exclaimed. 'Who says that the laird's condition is a question of poisoning?'

'Why, now, I had heard that it was you,' he said blandly.

I was becoming more annoyed by the minute. I rose and went through to Mrs Mackintosh's kitchen, where I commissioned a pot of tea, before going upstairs to deposit my medical bag and wash up. By the time I had done these things I was a little cooler, but still irritated by the intervention of this suspicious foreigner. I descended the stairs with my mind made up to send Macleod away with a flea in his ear.

I began my remarks as I opened the sitting-room door.

'Now, look here, Macleod, this really will not do—'

I was interrupted by a familiar voice. 'I'm sure you're right, Watson,' said the voice of Sherlock Holmes, 'but never fear, your irritating American acquaintance has gone.'

My speech died on my tongue and I stepped into the room to find Holmes sprawled in the armchair where Macleod had sat minutes before. The blue spectacles, the side whiskers and the silvering hair were all gone, but the clothes were still those of the fictitious musician.

'Holmes!' I complained. 'You have done it again!'

He laughed. 'So I have,' he admitted, 'but you must not berate me. You know how I enjoy my little theatrical interludes, and besides, I have acquired some useful information. Now, give me a moment to change out of Macleod's clothing and I would like to discuss Czernowski-Stuart's condition with you.'

He was upstairs in a flash and back as soon. Mrs Mackintosh brought in the tea and expressed her amazement at seeing Holmes.

'Did you just come back from the station?' she asked. 'I brought a cup for the American gentleman, but I see he's gone, so it'll do for you.'

So she served our tea, while Holmes grinned at me childishly from behind her. When we were served and she had withdrawn, Holmes became all business.

'Tell me what has been going on in Strathcullar in my imagined absence, Watson,' he asked.

'I should have thought,' I said, a little huffily, 'that your crony at the inn would have kept you informed.'

'Some of it, certainly, but I would still wish to hear your account, my friend.'

As quickly and succinctly as possible I filled him in on events, from the laird's mysterious illness to the bizarre events by night on Inish Beg. He heard me out silently with an expressionless face.

'Let me deal with your report in reverse, if I may, Watson,' he said when I had finished. 'Firstly, let us consider your experiences at the graveyard.'

'I assure you that every word of it is true,' I said. 'Young Lacky will bear me witness.'

'There are two things here, Watson. The first is the light which Lacky saw on the previous night. You, quite correctly, told him that it could not be any ghost or bogle, but a living person, and determined to investigate. Your investigation served its purpose far enough to confirm your original deduction: namely that the light which Lacky saw was real and was born by a human hand. You saw that person carrying out a careful inspection of the gravestones on Inish Beg. That was well done, Watson, and I applaud your efforts. We know now that a tall resident of this village maintains an interest in the little island which he does not wish to be generally known. I think we may say, also, that he is an outsider to the village. You have described Lacky's objections to Inish Beg at night. I imagine any other native would feel the same reservations.'

'Thank you,' I said. 'But what about the other?'

'Ah,' he said, and drew on his pipe, 'the other.'

There was a longish pause while I awaited his explanation of the horror I had witnessed on the island.

'Imagine,' he said at last, 'someone else who was on Inish Beg on that night, someone who, like you, wished to know if there was somebody visiting the island at night. They might have hidden in the little mortuary until it was dark, then waited for the intruder to arrive. Sure enough, the expected visitor manifests and begins his inspection of the gravestones. Totally unexpected, two more visitors arrive – yourself and young Lacky. The original intruder's search begins to take him towards the mortuary and you and Lacky begin to creep in behind him. Was that not the situation you described?'

'It was,' I agreed. 'But who on earth would have been in the mortuary?'

He ignored my question. 'The observer in the mortuary,' he went on, 'would have been in grave danger of discovery, Watson. Imagine him, already dressed darkly and hidden in the shadow of the mortuary's doorway, suddenly displaying his hands, covered with a theatrical phosphorescent mixture, and emitting a strange noise. When that proved insufficient to hold the intruder at bay, he spread the mixture on his face and produced a skull-like appearance, which was sufficient to unnerve the gravestone inspector completely.'

'That,' I said, 'is as preposterous an explanation as that it was a ghost that we saw. You disappoint me, Holmes.'

'Nevertheless,' he said quietly, 'that is precisely what I did.'

It was seconds before his words penetrated properly.

'You!' I exclaimed. 'What in Heaven's name were you doing on Inish Beg at night?'

'The same as your good self,' he said. 'Seeking to know who it was that maintained a secret interest in the island. On the previous night I had been smoking a pipe at my bedroom window after the inn closed, when I saw the same light that Lacky must have seen. I decided to try and observe the explorer, because I, too, am developing an interest in that island. I did not wish to take one of the boats, which would have made my purposes obvious, so I wrapped a few necessaries in oilskin and swam out early the next morning.'

'You swam out!' I repeated.

'It is no great distance and the water is warm. I laid up in the mortuary all day and, late at night, a boat grounded on the shingle. I was congratulating myself when I realized that the arrivals were you and Lacky, followed fairly closely by my real target. After that, events took the course which you witnessed. Subsequently I waited until you had returned to the jetty and swam back to the village.'

I was dumbfounded and could devise no appropriate comment. There were times in our relationship when I really believed that Holmes was taking advantage of our friendship by playing upon my emotions for his own amusement. I believed that this was one of them. He had come to me as Dr Macleod and raised in me a certain pitch of irritation with the man before revealing himself, and now he sat calmly before me and admitted that while Lacky had been praying for his soul and I had been considering firing at the dreadful thing that confronted us, he had been playing music hall tricks with phosphorus.

After a long silence Holmes said, 'Imagine my quandary once the intruder had fled. I have never questioned your courage, but I have often had occasion to doubt your logic. I did not know whether you believed that I was a ghost and could not, therefore, be harmed by a bullet, or whether, not knowing what you were witnessing, you might decide to test the situation with a shot. These considerations ran through my mind while you pointed your loaded pistol at me, finally convincing me to disappear rapidly.'

My temper melted away and I laughed. 'Holmes,' I said, 'the music halls lost a great possibility when you took to detection as a profession.'

'It is kind of you to say so, and I did once consider a theatrical career, but I convinced myself that other things are more important – speaking of which, Watson,' he said, 'I gather that our friend's condition is serious and that you suspect poisoning. Would you be so good as to recite the symptoms?'

Quickly I ran over the matters which had been foremost in my mind for days. When I had done he pulled out his briar pipe and lit it, smoking it reflectively for several minutes

214

with his eyes half-closed. I had been longing for his opinion on the matter, but when he took note of me again he was as cryptic as ever.

'Tonight,' he said, 'you and I have a little resurrection work to do.'

'Resurrection work!' I exclaimed. 'Surely we're not going to exhume Tam Chater? Or are we going to Inish Beg again?'

'I do not propose to commit a crime, Watson, but there is a resurrection which we must effect, and it is not upon Inish Beg.'

'But what about the laird's condition?'

'I shall be in a better position to advise you when we have completed our expedition,' he said, 'and that cannot take place until after the inn has closed tonight.'

He drew from his pocket a letter and slit the envelope with his pocketknife. I could see that the document inside was a long one, accompanied by diagrams. From the expression on Holmes' face he seemed to be well pleased with the contents.

'What have you there?' I asked eventually.

'Some more fruits of our labours, Watson. Do not think that the day we spent wandering about the loch, paddling through swamps and traipsing up the pass, was fruitless. Since I did not, in fact, go to Edinburgh, I had to send my observations by post, and here is a reply from the university, making clear that I am thinking along the right lines. Now, the food at the inn is well enough, but it falls far short of our good landlady's table. Do you think it is time for luncheon yet?'

He made no further reference to the inquiry in hand, but chatted amiably over our meal, and during the afternoon, his conversation ran across a wide range of topics including mediaeval music, the laws of inheritance, the forthcoming coronation of King Edward and the mechanics of the internal combustion engine.

The evening he spent with his maps and the letter from Edinburgh, drawing new diagrams and making fresh calculations. It was well after dark when we heard Ewan Breck at the jetty hailing Lacky to take him back to the castle. Moments later the last straggler wandered past our window, singing unintelligibly to himself, on the way home from the inn. Then the village fell silent.

Holmes consulted his watch. 'Fetch the dark lantern and bring your pistol,' he said. 'The game's afoot.'

Resurrection Men

Our landlady had retired, so we slipped silently out of the backdoor. I stood and awaited my friend's instructions, for I had not the least idea where we were going.

Holmes slid into Mrs Mackintosh's garden shed and emerged with a small spade.

'Now,' he whispered, 'that we are fully equipped, let us set about our grim task.' And he set off along the footpath that led across the back of the village gardens.

I thought that his attitude seemed unduly frivolous if we really were about to exhume a body but, assuming as ever that he had some realistic purpose in mind, I followed him along the pitch-dark path.

We had gone only a few yards when I realized that Holmes was counting the houses under his breath. After a short while he stopped and whispered, 'It is this one,' indicating a back gate beside the footpath.

He silently lifted the loop of string which held the gate closed, easing it back on its hinges, and we slid into the garden.

'Light the dark lantern,' he commanded, 'but keep it low.'

I applied a vesta to the lantern's wick and kept the slide almost shut.

'Now,' said Holmes, 'there are no lights on this side of the house, so we are not observed. You will oblige me by placing the lantern on the ground and rotating it slowly.'

I did as instructed, and the thin sliver of light showed us that the garden was ill-kempt, covered principally in scrubby grass. Holmes watched the lantern's beam as it slid across the grass. Suddenly he grasped my arm.

'There it is!' he exclaimed. 'Do you see?'

I could see that the lantern's beam was now throwing a long shadow in front of it, where its light had struck a rise in the ground.

'Is that a grave?' I asked.

'I imagine so,' said Holmes, and he gently applied his spade to the mound.

The cautious removal of only a few shovels full of soil proved him right. Something which was once alive lay shallowly under the soil and the warm spring air was now ripe with the odour of decay.

Holmes paused and knelt beside the hole he had dug.

'Shine the light here!' he commanded.

I released the shutter a little further and

shone the light on the ground at Holmes' feet. I was relieved but perplexed to see that the depression in the soil was taken up by the corpse of a large and elderly mongrel dog. I recognized it instantly as Ewan Breck's former companion.

'That's Breck's old dog, Jock,' I said. 'It became ill and Breck couldn't bring himself to destroy it. Fisher shot it.'

'Indeed,' agreed Holmes. 'Breck told me, but he did not tell me that somebody gutted the poor beast after it was shot,' and he pointed.

It was certainly clear that the animal had been killed with a single large-calibre bullet to the head. It was equally obvious that it had been gutted after death.

'Who on earth would want to do that?' I said. 'Surely not Breck?'

'Certainly not,' said Holmes, and began to shovel earth back over the animal's mangled remains.

A mechanical click sounded like a shot in the still darkness. I realized that it was the latch of a back door opening and in an instant I doused the lantern and flung myself outstretched behind a clump of weeds by the fence. Holmes dropped at my side.

The backdoor opened and a figure stood on the doorstep, though it was too dark to identify anyone. From within the house a female voice spoke.

The unmistakeable tones of Seamus Fisher replied. 'Give us the lantern here!' he commanded, and a light wavered in the doorway before he lifted a lamp over his head and began to peer about the yard. I was gratified to note that Fisher was in carpet slippers, but if he chose to step down the yard we would be hard put to it to escape without being recognized.

The woman's voice spoke again in the house and Fisher replied. 'It's cats,' he said, 'after poor old Jock's remains, the dirty brutes.'

Holmes chose to reinforce Fisher's view by emitting a highly realistic meow. Fisher stooped and picked up something from the ground by the doorstep. A moment later we were showered with a fistful of small stones.

Suddenly a most peculiar sound came from the mouth of Sherlock Holmes, a kind of strangled snarling and hissing sound. Seamus drew back on the doorstep, then stepped quickly inside and shut the door.

We could hear him calling to the woman, 'Quick! Fetch Tam's gun!'

'Now, Watson!' hissed Holmes in my ear, and in a flash we were on our feet and slipping silently out of the gate. As we stepped quickly along the footpath we heard the Irishman come out into the yard again, calling to the woman that he was right.

It was not very long before we had replaced the spade and were back in the parlour of our lodgings. Holmes dropped into an armchair with a grim smile.

'A useful night's work, Watson,' he remarked.

'What on earth,' I asked, 'was that strange snarling noise that you emitted back there?'

He laughed. 'I pride myself,' he said, 'that it was a reasonably lifelike imitation of the sound of a Scottish wildcat when annoyed by a handful of gravel. It was, in any case, realistic enough to persuade Fisher not to venture down a dark garden where one might be lurking until he had a weapon.'

'It was as well for us,' I observed, 'that he did not come to the door with Chater's pistol the first time around!'

Holmes lifted an eyebrow. 'You would save a great deal of energy, Watson, if you confined yourself to thinking about situations as they actually are or realistically might be, instead of wasting effort on what they could have been but weren't.'

He drew his pipe from his pocket and lit it. 'Be a good fellow,' he said, 'and pop into the kitchen. I think we deserve a pot of tea, then a last pipe and bed. We have both to visit the laird in the morning.'

I did as he suggested and, as we sipped the

brew, asked, 'Why must we both go to the castle tomorrow?'

'Because,' he said, 'I believe you are right. The laird is being poisoned and, subject to anything which Mrs Herd can tell me, I believe I know by whom.'

Morning saw us accompanying Guthrie to the castle. Breck met us at the door and was about to escort us to the laird's bedroom when Holmes announced that he wished to see Mrs Herd, so the old man led us through the castle to the kitchen, a large room at the rear of the ground floor with a stone-flagged floor, an enormous cast-iron range and a huge deal table.

Mrs Herd sat by the great table with the parlourmaid, both of them sipping tea. Surprised as she was by our sudden appearance in her domain, she soon had us all seated about the table with tea and a plate of scones before us, though all of us had not long broken our fast.

'I take it,' said Guthrie, 'that the laird has not improved, Mrs Herd?'

She shook her head. 'Not at all,' she said. 'He still cannae keep anything solid down, and he hasnae even taken my good broth for a day or two.'

'I believe,' said Holmes, 'that the laird's illness commenced from the morning after a dinner of haggis?'

'That's right,' she confirmed. 'He's awfy fond of the haggis and I gave him a good plateful with neeps and tatties.'

'Haggis with turnip and potatoes,' translated Holmes. 'And you would be quite sure that there was nothing wrong with the haggis or the vegetables?'

'Not at all,' she said. 'The vegetables were all fresh-grown hereabouts and the haggis I made myself.'

Holmes nodded. 'Forgive a mere Englishman, Mrs Herd, but I have eaten and enjoyed haggis many times without being quite sure how it is made. What goes into it?'

'Well now, when you come down to it, a haggis is just a sort of big sausage. It's made of minced meat and oats and barley and herbs and maybe a wee touch of spice, all stuffed into the pluck of a sheep to make a big pudding of it.'

My friend nodded again. 'And what meat went into the haggis the night before the laird was taken ill?'

'It was a deer's liver,' she said. 'Ewan Breck brought it to me. He said that Seamus the ganger had come across a young buck on the hills that had broken its leg and that he had to shoot it.'

Holmes nodded for a third time. 'And did you not think it odd that Mr Fisher did not send you any more of the animal's meat?'

'No,' she said. 'He's probably kept that for himself or sold it at the inn, but he's a man who seeks favours, so I suppose he thought that a nice piece of liver for the laird's haggis would be remembered.'

'What did you do with the liver? Was it all minced up for the haggis?'

It was the housekeeper's turn to shake her head. 'No,' she said. 'That would make the haggis mixture too rich and heavy. I minced it all and some went intae the haggis, but the rest I put in the pot to make a good strong broth.'

'Do you have any of that broth left?' asked Holmes.

'Aye,' she said, and pointed to where a large black pot stood on the range. 'Like I say, the laird cannae even take the broth noo, so I was going to throw it away.'

Holmes got up and stepped up to the range. Lifting the lid of the large pot, he took a spoon and sipped a small sample of the broth, turning it round in his mouth like a wine-taster. When he returned to the table his face was grim.

'You would be well advised to follow your instinct and destroy that broth,' he said.

Mrs Herd looked startled. 'You're not saying that there's something wrong with it?'

'Your broth tastes excellent,' said Holmes,

'as I expected it to. There is no hint that anything in it is not fresh, but nevertheless, there is something in it which is the cause of the laird's condition.'

'But if the vegetables were all fresh and the liver was all right—' she began, but Holmes raised a hand to silence her.

'There is nothing wrong apart from the fact that Seamus Fisher lied about that liver. It was not from a young deer, but from a very elderly dog called Jock.'

'A dog's liver!' exclaimed Guthrie and Mrs Herd together.

'So it was,' said Holmes.

'But surely,' said Guthrie, 'ingesting dog meat should not poison him. Have I not heard or read that the Chinese eat dogs?'

'So they may,' said Holmes, 'but the Esquimaux will not eat the liver of their huskies, even when forced by circumstances to eat dog meat. It seems that something in a dog's liver is harmful to man, and the older the dog the more harm is done.'

'But where would Fisher come by that information?' I asked.

'From his chum Breck,' said Holmes. 'Ewan Breck has lived and worked above the snowline and driven huskies. He told us so. As a matter of fact, it may have been from Chater, who had similar experience.'

'Are you saying that Seamus has tried to

poison the laird?'

'I am indeed, Watson. And I must ask all of you here to say nothing of this to anyone. I shall deal with Mr Fisher in due course. You, Guthrie, may explain the situation to Mr Czernowski-Stuart and you and Watson must put your heads together and derive a regimen which may undo the damage to the laird.'

To Inish Beg Again

Holmes and I returned to our lodgings. I had been astounded by my friend's diagnosis of the cause and means of the poisoning of the laird, but also profoundly grateful for a solution. I was still concerned that Czernowski-Stuart's health had been so undermined by Fisher's evil device that the laird might yet not recover. Still, Guthrie and I had agreed a regimen which we hoped would flush the poison from his system and build him up and all we could now do was watch and wait.

Over luncheon I asked Holmes, 'What are you going to do about Fisher now?'

'The poisoning of the laird makes it clear that he is a killer, and the other indications make a circumstantial case against him as the killer of Carter and McNair. Nevertheless, I would not care to be the advocate who argued an attempted poisoning case before a Scots jury in the High Court based on the folklore of the Esquimaux of Canada. Never forget that Scotland has the third verdict of "Not Proven", and I fear that would be the result. As to the London murders, there is, as yet, no clear evidence against him. So I shall continue to act as before – to go about my inquiries and researches very publicly, in the hope that it will lure Fisher into precipitate action. So far it seems to be an effective policy.'

'How do you mean?' I asked.

'The poisoning of Czernowski-Stuart is, in itself, evidence of the onset of panic on Fisher's part. He evidently fears that I am drawing close to solving the puzzle of the American gold, and, not knowing for whom we act, fears that I shall hand the secret of the gold to the laird. Whether Seamus acts of his own greed or – which I believe to be more likely – as an agent of the American conspiracy, he would not want that to happen, so he has attempted to remove the laird from the equation.'

I nodded. 'And are you?' I said.

'Am I what, Watson?'

'Are you close to finding the gold?'

'I believe so, Watson, I believe so. If this were Baker Street I might suggest that you take a Turkish bath or a game of billiards. As it is, I shall be grateful if you will amuse yourself with a book this afternoon, or take a stroll. I must apply myself to the information received from Edinburgh.'

Realizing that he wished to be left undisturbed, I settled down after luncheon with a book, while Holmes attacked his papers, notes and diagrams.

Teatime came, and Holmes was forced to clear space on the table for our repast, but returned to his labours as soon as the meal was over.

Mrs Mackintosh had long lit the lamps before my friend withdrew to an armchair and dropped into it with a contented sigh.

'You are making progress?' I asked.

He lit his pipe and inhaled deeply. 'I believe that I have made a great deal of progress,' he said. 'If I am right, I shall soon be able to locate within inches the hiding place of the American angels. We must, however, make another brief expedition to Inish Beg to complete my data. We can do that after you visit the laird in the morning.'

I was anxious to see the patient in the morning, and pleased when I did so. Not only was his pulse stronger and more regular, but his voice seemed to have strengthened and I thought I saw a hint of colour returning to his wan cheeks.

'I could wish for a more varied diet than thick vegetable soup, fruit cordials and stimulants,' he complained, 'but I should thank you and Guthrie for pulling me round.'

'You should rather thank your own excellent constitution for beginning to reject the poisonous broth, and Sherlock Holmes for putting his finger on the cause. As to pulling round, while I detect signs of improvement, it is still an uphill road for you.'

Nevertheless, I now believed that, with luck and provided that he did nothing foolish, our patient would survive.

Lacky dropped Guthrie at the jetty and took Holmes and I on to the little graveyard island. Holmes paced about the island with his stick, pointing out to me indications of my last visit.

'There,' he indicated, 'is where you and Lacky came over the wall, and here,' and he pointed with his stick again, 'is where our intruder stood and faced me. A tall, heavy man with a limp, Watson. Perhaps our Regent's Park killer, eh?'

Soon I was at large while Holmes busied himself with measurements by compass. From the eastern shore he took a bearing on the Pictish stone on the hillside, marking a spot on the shore with a fragment of dead branch thrust into the ground. Then he went to the western shore and took a bearing on the spot where his handkerchief flag still fluttered beside the thicket and the swamp, marking that point with another branch. It was at about this point that I noticed a boat setting out from the jetty and making towards Inish Beg. As it drew nearer I could see that it was manned only by Ewan Breck.

'We have a visitor, Holmes,' I said, and drew his attention to the boat.

'So we have,' he said. 'We have also an observer, who is, as before, watching our operations through field glasses. Would it surprise you to note that the reflection of the glasses comes from the hillside, above and behind Fisher's lodging? I suggest that we take our refreshment now, Watson.'

So it was that the old man came ashore to find Holmes and I seated on boulders that marked ancient graves while we ate our provisions.

'Mr Breck!' Holmes hailed him. 'What brings you to Inish Beg?'

Breck looked about him, a trifle nervously I thought. 'Oh, I've no' so much to do with the laird being ill. Jessie and Mrs Herd can mind to him until he's up and aboot again, so it crossed my mind to come and look at the wee island here.'

'Do you come here often?' I enquired.

He shook his head. 'Only noo and again, and that's by daylight. I wouldnae set foot here at night,' he said.

'Afraid of ghosts?' I ventured.

'There's all sorts buried here,' he said, 'heathens and murderers and suicides. I

231

wouldnae say that they do walk, but if they do I've nae intention of meeting them.'

We laughed. 'So you make a visit now and then in daylight,' pursued Holmes.

'Aye. I like to look about and reflect on the shortness of the years of man and the ways that he comes to his end.'

Holmes looked about him. 'I imagine,' he said, 'that the most pathetic graves here are those of the tinkers. Did Mungo Breck carve their stones?'

'Aye,' said the old man. 'It was long before my time of course, but Mungo Breck was an ancestor of mine and the old folks used to tell how Mungo said that they were Christians cut down in misfortune, that we'd buried them among pagans and murderers, but they deserved a proper memorial, even if naebody knew their names.'

Holmes nodded. 'I have heard that your ancestor Mungo was involved in the hiding of the gold that came from France. Is that so?'

'You'll hear a wonderful heap of tales about that gold,' said Breck, 'but that's what the family always said. He was a clever man, was Mungo, a verra clever man, so I don't doubt he'd have had to dae with it.'

'Did he not leave any clue?' I asked, while Holmes gave me a covert frown.

'Folk who know that I'm Mungo's kin

always ask me that,' he said. 'All I can say is that my father told me that it was all in the painting, you ken – the big picture he painted for the castle.'

'Was there not,' said Holmes, 'a silly rhyme about the gold?'

'Oh aye,' said Breck. 'We used to sing it in the schoolyard. Let me see, I think it went like this.'

He sang a couple of verses to an air similar to 'For He's a Jolly Good Fellow':

'Where is Bonnie Prince Charlie?
Where is Bonnie Prince Charlie?
Where is Bonnie Prince Charlie?
And who has got his gold?
Prince Charlie's gone to Heaven,
Prince Charlie's gone to Heaven,
Prince Charlie's gone to Heaven,
And someone's got his gold.
Ask the Picts and the tinklers,
Ask the Picts and the tinklers,
Ask the Picts and the tinklers,
Who's got Prince Charlie's gold...'

He faltered to a stop.

'Was there not another verse?' said Holmes.

'Aye, I think there was, but I cannae just recall it.'

He lifted a farewell hand to us and wandered off towards the small stone mortuary. Holmes began his compass observations again, now taking bearings from each of his marked points on the shore to the other. While he was about this, Breck emerged from the little stone mortuary and wished us good day as he returned to his boat and pulled for the village.

Holmes now paced out a path from one marker to the other, turning at the end to look back. When he had done so, he came and sat back on the boulder beside me.

'Did you notice, Watson,' he asked, 'that the path between my two markers on the shore avoided every single one of the many burials on this island?'

'As a matter of fact, I did,' I said. 'But it passed through the middle of the row of gypsy graves.'

'So it did,' he agreed. 'Between the third and fourth stones.'

'And that means something?' I said.

'It means,' he said, 'that I can be almost certain as to the location of the American gold. It remains only to trap the murderous Fisher.'

While we waited for Lacky to return for us, Holmes dug into the knapsacks again, seeking the remains of our food, and ate heartily. That was always a clear sign that he believed an inquiry was progressing satisfactorily.

As Lacky rowed us back to shore, Holmes

asked, 'Do you remember a playground rhyme about Prince Charlie's gold, Lacky?'

'Oh aye,' said the boy. 'There was a daft thing that the girls used to sing for skipping to.' He sang the lines that Breck had sung, but added another two verses:

'King George's men they sought it,
King George's men they sought it,
King George's men they sought it,
And never found a penny.
'The gold is with the angels,
The gold is with the angels,
The gold is with the angels,
And so's Prince Charlie too.'

'Well done, Lacky,' said Holmes. 'You're right that it's silly. The piece about the gold being with the angels is a confusion. The gold was minted in coins called "angels".'

The boy's jaw dropped. 'You mean that there really was a lot of gold, Mr Holmes?'

'There was indeed, Lacky, and I believe it is still here.'

Turning aside, Holmes muttered to me, 'That should reach our target and ensure that he knows that I've found the gold.'

Nocturnal Adventures Again

Holmes was at his conversational and affable best when we arrived back at our lodgings. I had observed the effect on many occasions; although our inquiry was not complete, my friend had now solved all the major problems that had confronted him and could see his way to the end.

It was, accordingly, a pleasant evening and I retired to my bed in a relaxed frame of mind. On the street below our window we heard the inn's last stragglers wander past, followed by silence.

We were both, I think, about to drop off, when there was another sound of footsteps in the road and two voices, seemingly in argument. They, too, passed away, and I was almost asleep when a brisk rattle sounded at our window. For a moment I thought it was wind-driven rain, but then my mind cleared and I realized that someone was flinging gravel at the pane.

A second burst followed quickly on the first.

'Holmes,' I said, 'someone below is trying to attract our attention.'

I had thought him asleep, but he sprang from his bed in one move, slipping on his dressing gown and stepping to the window. As I struggled to follow him, the window was opened and I could hear Lacky's voice in a loud whisper from below.

'Go and knock up the police officers at the inn!' Holmes commanded the boy. 'Then all three of you join us at the jetty.'

He closed the window and swung round to me. 'Quickly, Watson!' he said. 'Get some clothes on, and we shall need your pistol and the dark lantern.'

In a very short time we were both dressed and downstairs. We let ourselves out quietly by the back door and rounded the house, making for the jetty. Once there I had my first opportunity to question Holmes.

'Lacky says that Fisher and Alan Breck have taken a boat to Inish Beg. The old man seems to have been going under protest and Fisher was holding a gun on him. The boy saw them from his bedroom window,' Holmes explained.

'What are your plans?' I asked.

'Ill-formed at present,' he said. 'I need to know if either of our policemen can row reasonably, and I need to consult young Lacky.'

Within moments the three arrived from the inn. Holmes gave the officers a brief outline of the situation. It turned out that both of them could handle an oar. He turned, then, to Lacky.

'If you row us to Inish Beg,' he said, 'Fisher will hear us coming, and he is armed. Can you think of a way we can get there silently?'

The youth thought for a moment, then he said, 'The river current sets to the north of Inish Mor and Inish Beg. If we go northeast of the castle, we can run down on Inish Mor with the current, without using the oars. I might have to steer her a bit for the last few yards, but they shouldnae hear us coming.'

'Excellent!' said Holmes. 'Now, if our two inspectors will give us time to pass the castle, then start out in another boat, that will serve as a distraction if Fisher becomes aware of them.'

'You say this Fisher is armed?' said Mc-Brain.

'He has a revolver,' said Holmes, 'though I do not know how expert he may be. On the other hand, he probably has at least one knife and is an expert thrower.'

'Do you expect us to land on the island?' asked Hopkins.

'I hope,' said Holmes, 'that when Fisher hears you coming it will distract him sufficiently for Watson and I to take action. Now, Lacky, let us away!'

We tumbled down the steps and were soon pulling away from the shore, while Hopkins and McBrain occupied another boat.

Our operations would have been pointless had there been a moon, but the night was inky. Not a whisper of air disturbed the water and, as Lacky pulled out strongly, we slid along the surface as though riding on black glass.

We passed the castle on our right and, after a minute, we could tell by the sound of Lacky's oars and the movements of the boat that we had picked up the river current running through the loch. Lacky shipped one oar and put the other over the stern to act as a rudder.

For some time we glided silently across the smooth black water and I peered ahead, seeking any sign of our destination, but the little cemetery island seemed to be invisible in the gloom. Then a light flared, somewhere ahead of us.

'They have lit a lantern,' I whispered to Holmes, conscious of the way in which voices travel across water.

'A dark lantern, I imagine,' he murmured, and, sure enough, a second later the light vanished as someone shut the lantern's slide.

Soon we could hear Fisher's voice and a second voice replying to him. Lacky's stern oar turned us towards Inish Beg and Holmes asked him, 'Can you turn us in to the far side of the island, behind the little mortuary building? That seems to be the best place for us to try and land unseen, since they seem to be this side.'

Lacky nodded and, by careful manoeuvres of his temporary rudder, took us along the side of the island and brought us up behind the little mortuary.

'Now,' said Holmes, 'do not touch the shingle. They will hear it. We shall wade ashore quietly.' Turning to Lacky, he said, 'You stay in the boat and make yourself inconspicuous. Under no circumstances should you set foot ashore unless Watson or I call you by name.'

As the lad steadied the boat, Holmes and I stepped over the side and waded carefully to the little beach. We could hear Fisher and Breck arguing at the other side of the island, and had no difficulty in reaching the shelter of the mortuary without their detecting us.

Once inside the building, we were able to stand side by side at the one window, which was beside the door and looked across the middle of the island. The thick stonework of which the mortuary was constructed enabled us to watch from the window while our faces lay in deep shadow, but the darkness of the night was such that we could see very little.

We did see their lantern flash briefly close to the farther shore.

'Fisher is examining my markers,' whispered Holmes. 'They will not help him unless he has worked the thing out for himself. Somehow I doubt that.'

Breck's voice reached us. 'He put markers each side of the island,' he said. 'Why do you think he did that?'

'I don't know,' replied Fisher. 'They only mark an east to west line. I don't see what help that is.'

'They have a compass,' whispered Holmes.

'I thought you had some kind of a clue?' Breck complained.

'I did, but it's damaged,' said Fisher. 'You were here today while Holmes was fooling about. I saw you talking to them. What did they say?'

'They asked me if my ancestor left any clue.'

'What did you tell them?'

'Only what I've told folk for years, that the only thing my family remembered was that there was supposed to be a clue in the big painting at the castle.'

Fisher snorted. 'Humph! That's no earthly

help. That damned picture shows the whole valley, just about everywhere the gold could possibly be. What else did they say?'

'Mr Holmes asked me if there wasnae a song aboot the gold. He meant that silly auld thing that the bairns still sing in the schoolyard.'

'That's no help, either,' said Fisher. 'Did he say why he thought it was on Inish Beg?'

'Of course he didnae.' He only wanted to know if I knew anything. Can we be oot of here now, Seamus? This place fair gives me the shivers at night.'

I heard a metallic sound that told me the Irishman had laid his pistol on one of the tombs.

'No,' he said, 'we can't go. Holmes made his measurements from each end of the loch and now he's picked on Inish Beg. He must think its here somewhere for sure. He's a pretty smart fellow by all accounts.'

The stars were giving a faint light which, reflected from the water, enabled us to see a little better. I could see that Seamus was searching his pockets for something. At last he took out what seemed to be a piece of paper.

'Hold up the lantern!' he commanded Breck.

The old man did so and let a narrow thread of light escape. Fisher held up the paper and peered closely at it.

'It's no use,' he said, after a moment. 'I can only read one line of it.'

'What is it?' asked Breck.

'It's the reason I'm certain the gold is here. It's a clue that McNair found in the castle. He gave Tam Chater a copy, but it's been spoiled. All I can see is a bit which says, "where the forgotten lie". That's got to be here, hasn't it? Where the forgotten lie must mean where the folk nobody wants to remember are buried.'

'Whisht!' exclaimed his companion. 'There's a boat coming over from the village. You dinnae think it's the polis, do you?'

'It's more likely that interfering busybody Holmes,' snarled his companion. 'I swear I'll give him a hot welcome if he tries to land here!'

'Listeners,' whispered Holmes, 'hear no good of themselves. Only a moment past I was a pretty smart fellow.'

The two men outside were both looking across the water. Fisher had dropped his piece of paper.

'What's this?' said Breck, picking up the crumpled sheet. 'This is all covered in blood! Where have you had it from?'

There was a pause, and we could tell that the truth was dawning on Breck. Suddenly he snatched Fisher's pistol from the tomb-stone.

'You killed him, didn't you, you murder-ing scoundrel! You murdered Tam Chater for that piece of paper!'

He jerked up the lantern and the slide opened, illuminating Fisher, who had turn-ed, startled, to face the angry Scot.

'I swore I'd be the death of whoever killed Tam Chater, if I had to do it with my ain hands,' shouted Breck, and he raised the pistol.

We had to intervene or stand by and see murder done. I whipped my Adams from my pocket and took aim, but Fisher lunged at Breck and the lantern went flying, falling to the ground and lighting what followed with an eerie underglow.

Fisher and the old man wrestled for the gun, but I saw the Irishman's hand slip into his coat. He was evidently reaching for a knife. There was no more time. As soon as I could do so without harming Breck, I fired. Both men fell simultaneously.

Grabbing our own lantern, Holmes and I plunged from the mortuary, rushing to the spot where the two had fallen. I could see immediately that I had shot too well. I had not just disabled Fisher, but killed him. Holmes knelt by Breck, who was curled on the ground, clutching a fearful gash in his belly from which blood was pouring. A skean-dhu lay beside him.

Quickly I used the knife to slice away portions of the dead Irishman's shirt, attempting to staunch the flow of blood from the old man's wound.

'Holmes,' I urged, 'call Lacky and the inspectors. This man is dreadfully wounded. We must get him to the castle as swiftly as possible!'

Holmes stood and shouted for our reinforcements and soon all three arrived.

'Good Heavens, Mr Holmes!' exclaimed Hopkins. 'We were just pulling ashore when we heard the shot. What's been happening?'

'There's no time for explanations,' snapped Holmes. 'Breck is injured, and your killer lies there.' He pointed to Fisher's body. 'As soon as Watson can stem the bleeding we must take the old man to the castle. If you, Lacky and Watson ferry Breck across, McBrain and I will follow in one of the other boats.'

It was no mean matter to lodge Ewan Breck in Lacky's boat. Though I had padded and bound the wound as best I might with the materials available, his bandages were soaked with blood before we had him in the boat. As soon as he was aboard, Hopkins and Lacky took the oars and pulled as though the devil was behind us.

At Inish Mor Hopkins ran up to the castle and yanked on the great iron bell pull beside the door. Somewhere inside a bell sounded and soon lights sprang up. Hopkins returned and helped us carry Breck to the door-step.

Mrs Herd opened the door in night attire and curl papers, her hands flying to her face when she saw Breck's condition.

'Mercy!' she exclaimed. 'The puir man! You must bring him in!'

She led us through to a rear room with a large old-fashioned couch, where we were able to lay him. Soon she was ferrying hot water, towels and bandages from her kitchen or holding a lamp for me while I toiled over the silent old man.

I don't know how long it was before I straightened to ease my back. Sherlock Holmes stood by, a grim expression on his face.

'Will he live?' he asked.

I shook my head. 'I really do not know,' I said. 'I have, I think, stopped the bleeding, but it needs a surgeon to deal with any internal damage. It was a skilled and forceful thrust. He's not a young man and has led a hard life. He has resistance and willpower, but little strength, I fear.'

Sherlock Holmes Explains

For two days and nights I kept watch on poor Breck, using every skill that I possessed. I thought at one point that he would pull through, but an infection developed which I could not defeat. In the early hours of the third night he slipped away.

Before he died he managed one request – a message for the laird: 'Please tell His Highness I've always tried to be loyal.'

Holmes had reported on events to the laird, and reported to me that Czernowski-Stuart was much better and strengthening every day. A bedroom in the castle had been assigned to us and Holmes had fetched some of our belongings from Mrs Mackintosh's, so that I was able at last to lay myself in a comfortable bed and sleep the clock round.

It was Holmes who woke me at last with a cup of tea.

'Come, Watson,' he said, 'you cannot sleep through this evening. We are invited to dine.'

'To dine?' I said. 'With whom?'

'I have given Czernowski-Stuart only an outline of the events which led to Breck's death. Can you not imagine that, despite his grief for his old retainer, the laird is itching to know the entire story. You, I, the police officers and Guthrie are invited to share his board this evening.'

I started up in bed. 'He is not yet fit enough to eat a heavy dinner!' I protested.

'I suggest that you leave off doctoring for this evening. Besides, Guthrie will be there to keep an eye on him. For myself, I look forward to the event.'

A little later I was shaving in front of the mirror on our washstand. I found the stand too low, and had to stoop in an awkward position to see my own reflection.

'What are you doing, Watson?' asked Holmes.

'I am striving to achieve a clean shave in this infernal mirror,' I said. 'I cannot imagine how a man of your height manages. It seems a pity to me that Mr Mungo Breck, who knew so much about reflections, did not construct this washstand. He would have made it adjustable.'

Holmes was staring at me fixedly.

'Well done, Watson,' he said. 'That's the answer!'

'The answer to what?' I queried.

'To McNair's clue.'

'You mean that 718 thing?'

'No,' he said, dismissively. 'That is alphabetical. The seventh and eighteenth letters of the alphabet are G and R. They stand for "Golden Reflections".'

'But that's the name of the picture,' I said.

'Precisely, Watson. Now, do come on. It's almost dinnertime.'

So it was that we foregathered at the laird's table. The two police inspectors had borne him carefully downstairs and he sat in a great chair at the head of the board, wrapped in a fur robe and his head still bound, but looking and sounding a great deal healthier than when I saw him last.

As Jessie and Mrs Herd served the soup, the laird welcomed us all, taking the opportunity to make a very pretty little speech in the memory of Ewan Breck and ending with a complaint that he must sit and eat soup while his guests had the best of everything.

The meal progressed pleasantly until the dishes were cleared, when the laird addressed Guthrie and me.

'I take it,' he said, 'that neither of my two eminent medical guests have any objection to my indulging myself in a cigar and a tot of whisky?'

Guthrie and I looked at each other. 'A cigar maybe,' said Guthrie, 'but I'm not sure your constitution is strong enough for a good malt.'

I nodded agreement and our host scowled. 'I have been confined for days to vegetable soup, fruit cordials and stimulants,' he complained. 'What is malt whisky but the finest and purest restorative and stimulant in the world? Why did our ancestors call it the "water of life"?'

We chuckled, and agreed that he might allow himself a little leeway since his health was so much improved.

Mungo Breck's marvellously cunning drinks tray circulated, together with the elaborate cigar box. When we were all supplied the laird asked that we toast the memory of Ewan Breck, which we did.

When the toast was ended the laird put down his glass. 'Now, Mr Holmes, Dr Watson,' he said, 'while I have lain at death's door upstairs, it seems that you have been having some very strange adventures in my little fiefdom. I believe that the time has come to enlighten us all as to what has been happening.'

I looked at Holmes, who bowed his head modestly.

'You all know,' he began, 'the story of the French gold, intended for the American colonies in their forthcoming war against England, which was supposed to have been hidden somewhere in this vicinity and never found. Thanks to the laird, we know that it is true that such a shipment was made, and thanks to the research of the late Mr McNair, we know that the British Army, Navy and Revenue service sought the gold without success.'

He paused for a drink. 'So,' he went on, 'there has circulated, since the late eighteenth century, a story that a massive sum of gold angels bearing the imprint of Bonnie Prince Charlie was concealed somewhere in the vicinity of Strathcullar.

'More recently,' he continued, 'that tale reached the ears of two fortune hunters, Seamus Fisher and Tam Chater. It is probable that Chater had it from Ewan Breck when they camped and worked together in the Klondike. Fisher, I believe, may well have had it from another source. Chater was a fortune seeker who had tried his luck without success in Alaska and turned his sights to Strathcullar. Fisher was an Americanized Irishman who, at some point, if one can believe the tattoo he wore on his arm, was contacted by or contacted a seditious American organization, the purpose of which was to overthrow the government of the United States. They began that plan last year when, I am reliably informed, they were behind the assassination of President McKinley. To extend their influence they needed cash, and somehow they had heard of the Strathcullar hoard. Whether sent by them, or acting in his own interest, Fisher made his way here.'

He drank again. 'A third party then entered the picture. An Edinburgh lawyer, a clever but sharp practitioner, removed to Inverness, leaving debts behind him and embarking on a life which he could not afford. Soon he found himself appointed to manage our present host's affairs and making frequent visits to Strathcullar. A romantic interest in the Jacobite period led him to the story of the gold and he took full advantage of his situation. He searched the castle archives, drank with and questioned the natives and walked the vicinity in the company of that other fortune hunter, Tam Chater. At some point he found, in this building if we can believe the late Seamus Fisher, a clue to the whereabouts of the gold.'

He looked around the table. His audience was rapt.

'It was now that murder entered into the story. McNair realized that, even if he could obtain possession of the gold, he could never sell it. Accordingly, and probably through Chater, he made contact with an American. Whether he knew that he was dealing with an agent of the United States

Government I know not and am inclined to doubt, though it would not have mattered to him so long as the American would pay for the information.

'Seeking to keep his transactions well out of Scotland, he communicated with his American contact through a series of cryptic personal advertisements in a newspaper. It was those which attracted my attention and I was soon able to decipher them in the main. The element which I could not fathom was a series of numbers in the last exchange of messages and references to a "device". Thanks to the laird's collection, I now know that McNair was imitating a device which he had seen here – a series of transparent overlays which can be assembled to create a rough likeness of almost anyone, like a child's toy book. The numbers were to tell his contact in what order to assemble the transparencies so that recognition could be guaranteed when they met.'

'I would sue him for copyright, if my lawyer had not been murdered,' said the laird.

Holmes smiled. 'Certain aspects of those messages made me aware that whatever conspiracy was hatching, it had a Jacobite element, which I found singular. Consequently, when the messages arranged a meeting in Regent's Park, I determined that

253

Watson and I should be in the vicinity to see what mischief was afoot.'

He paused again for a drink. 'Unhappily, we were forestalled, and reached the park in time to find the murdered corpse of the American, Carter. He had been killed by a tall man, lame in one leg, who had shown extraordinary skill in throwing a skean-dhu. On the same afternoon, McNair was murdered at his hotel, also with a skean-dhu. Inspector Hopkins here became involved and he and I discussed the case. I remained puzzled by the apparent Jacobite connection and, having once known the laird's uncles, determined to visit Strathcullar and see what might be discovered. Before I could do so, I was approached by somebody else, whose identity I cannot disclose, and commissioned to find the killer of Carter and McNair and to locate the gold if at all possible.'

He looked at his empty glass. 'I have now, I believe, achieved both of those purposes and, if someone will pass the drinks tray, I shall be happy to tell you how.'

How Sherlock Holmes Did It

We refreshed our drinks and my friend continued.

'Watson and I had barely arrived here when Tam Chater took a potshot at me from the waterfall beside the eastern pass. Very shortly afterwards he was himself stabbed to death. I had theorized that he might have been slain by a fellow conspirator for drawing attention to himself. I observed at the time that something had been taken from his body, and I now know that to have been a copy of the clue apparently found in this castle by McNair. It may be that both reasons pertained. Certainly the killer was Seamus Fisher, who may also have been eliminating another rival for the gold.'

He paused again, and the laird interjected. 'You keep mentioning a clue which McNair found in the castle, Mr Holmes. What on earth was it?'

'It was a piece of verse,' said Holmes, 'but McNair's copy disappeared and Chater's was so damaged that only one line is decipherable. In any case, I had access to neither and had to take a different approach. Later I shall decipher the verse for you, by way of confirmation of my results.'

'What was your different approach?' asked Guthrie.

'Having no clues, I had to take them where I could find them. The first was that magnificent picture that hangs on the wall. When our host told Watson and I about Mungo Breck, it occurred to me that, with his intelligence, wit and skill, coupled with his radical Jacobitism, he would have been an ideal man to take part in, if not to lead, the concealment of the gold.'

He rose and walked to the picture. We turned to look.

'You will see, gentlemen, that this lovely work portrays almost the entire landscape of Strathcullar, the whole valley. It is painted from a very particular viewpoint and at a specific time of year. It shows the mid-summer sun setting in the cleft of the western mountains.'

We nodded, like students.

'Now the so-called Pictish stone by the eastern pass is not, of course, Pictish. It is a great deal older than the Pictish times. The ancient people who erected such monuments, as Sir Norman Lockyer has shown, frequently placed them in particular relationships to specific heavenly bodies at a certain time of year, one of which was midsummer. It seemed to me that the purpose of the stone was to act as what you might call a back sight, while another stone at the western end of the lake acted as a foresight, to establish a line across the landscape.'

'But what would be their purpose?' asked McBrain.

'To ensure that a person standing on the hillside could look across the loch and the distant stone and see if they lined up with the sun setting in the notch of the mountains. If they did, then he would know it was midsummer. They had no clocks and no calendars, but this was a perfectly reliable method.'

'Very clever,' said the laird, 'but I fail to see how it operates as a clue.'

'Its effect,' replied Holmes, 'is to mark a straight line across the landscape. Do you happen to possess a large-scale plan of the loch and its islands and a two-foot rule?'

'There's both in the top drawer of the chest to your left,' said our host.

Holmes opened the drawer and soon returned to his seat with a large plan and a rule. He spread the plan across the table so that we could all see it.

'Now,' he said, 'if the picture is truly a clue—'

'If the picture is a clue!' interrupted both

policemen, simultaneously, then grinned at each other. Holmes ignored them and continued.

'If the picture is a clue, then we can do this.'

He drew a mechanical pencil from his pocket and, seeking the location of the Pictish stone on the plan, drew a straight line across the loch to the smaller stone at the western end.

'How does that help?' asked McBrain.

'It narrows, by an enormous factor, the probable location of the gold,' said Holmes. 'You will observe that the line passes across the steep slope from the eastern pass, where nobody in their right mind would seek to haul a heavy cargo of gold, and then passes across the loch. It misses Inish Mor, which the Army would inevitably search, it misses all of the crannogs. It crosses only Inish Beg.'

'A graveyard,' said McBrain.

Holmes nodded. 'Indeed.'

'Surely, it might be in the loch,' said Hopkins, 'if all you're saying is that it's somewhere along that line?'

'It is not in the water,' said Holmes. 'Burgoyne's men dragged the loch and found nothing. Wherever it is, we require only one more thing.'

'What's that?' asked Guthrie.

'A second marker to indicate a point along that line.'

'And is there one?' asked the laird.

Holmes nodded. 'I believe that there is a very substantial and obvious one,' he said. 'How many of you have visited Inish Beg?'

All, of course, had, but the two police officers only briefly. Holmes explained for their benefit.

'There stand on Inish Beg,' continued Holmes, 'six handsome gravestones, apparently marking the graves of a family of unfortunate tinkers or gypsies, who were slain by an outbreak of fever, or cholera, or typhus or some such as they camped near Strathcullar. When I first visited the island I saw them, but I completely failed to understand their real significance. I observed that they were evidently designed and carved by Mungo Breck. I accepted fully the village story that Breck placed those stones as an act of Christian charity to an unfortunate group who had died namelessly and were forced to lie in the unhallowed soil of Inish Beg because the villagers feared infection. I failed to see the significance of the designs or of the singular placing of the stones.'

'What is significant about the designs?' I asked.

'They are decorated,' said Holmes, 'with angels and apple blossoms.'

'I can see that angels have a reference,' I said, 'but what about apple blossom?'

'Oh, Watson, Watson,' Holmes chided. 'The apple blossom, in Celtic legend, is the flower of the Blessed Isles, the land to which the happy dead go. And where is that land supposed to be? Beyond the Western Ocean, gentlemen. Beyond the Western Ocean, where Mungo Breck knew that the American colonies lay, a happy land seeking freedom from King George.'

'Far fetched,' opined McBrain, and Hopkins nodded.

'What else is singular about those stones, Mr Holmes?' asked our host.

Holmes smiled. 'I should have seen it the first time,' he said. 'Perhaps Dr Guthrie can tell us. Have you been on Inish Beg in the early morning or the evening, Doctor?'

Guthrie looked at him with puzzlement. 'I have sometimes been there early in the day, accompanying some lonely suicide to their unhallowed grave.'

He paused for thought, then realization dawned. 'By Heaven!' he said. 'I know what you mean! Those stones are back to front!'

'Back to front?' echoed Hopkins. 'How do you mean, Doctor?'

'Many of the burials on Inish Beg are not Christian interments. If they have a stone, it may face any way, but Christian gravestones are supposed to face the east, so that the resurrected may arise facing Jerusalem on the Day of Judgement. Those gypsy stones are supposed to be Christian, but they don't face east – they face west.'

'Precisely,' agreed Holmes. 'As though whatever is beneath them is expected to rise and travel westwards.'

Sherlock Holmes Proves his Case

There was a longish silence after Holmes' last comment, then McBrain spoke.

'I have tae observe,' he said, 'that I find your explanation ingenious, but reliant too much on connections which are non-existent or coincidental, or which you have imagined.'

I was appalled. None knew better than me the extent to which my friend disliked coincidence as an explanation. 'It is,' he has frequency said to me, 'the willing hand-maiden of a lazy mind.' To hear the Scots police officer accuse him of adopting co-incidence would have been very gall to him.

It was, I think, only the strictures of his situation at the laird's table that bore upon Holmes to restrain the sharp answer that such a sally would certainly have received at Baker Street.

His eyes flashed in the candle light and his mouth became a thin line, but all he said was, 'Coincidence indeed, Inspector McBrain? We shall see in due course. In the meantime, let me set out for you the methods by which I sought to identify the killer of Carter, McNair and Chater.'

He took a long swallow of whisky and began again.

'When Watson and I first came to Strathcullar my reasons for bringing us here were that the advertisements in London had clearly indicated to me a Jacobite connection. Having known our host's uncles, I knew that he was, most probably, as deeply immersed in the antiquity of Scotland as were his uncles and would have a claim to the Stuart throne. That suggested to me that I should consult him, apart from the fact that he had been a client of the luckless McNair.

'Before we set out,' he continued, 'we were informed of the question of the French gold. I have said that we came north with no consequential clues as to the whereabouts of the gold and precious little as to the killer.'

He sipped his drink. 'After arrival in Strathcullar we visited the inn, where we had the opportunity to observe most, if not all, of the adult males of the community. With very few exceptions they conform to the shorter type of Highlandman. Those who are taller lack the strength of shoulder that flung the knife into Carter's neck. That

263

is not to say that they lack general strength – I am sure that they will tramp and scramble for miles across moors, boulders and mountains – but they do not have the strongly developed arms of, say, a professional navvy.

'With this in mind,' he went on, 'I met, shortly afterwards, Ewan Breck and Seamus the ganger. Now Red Ewan was of a height that might match my suspect, but, again, would have lacked the strength of arm, apart from the fact that his eyesight was failing and his hands growing unsteady. Seamus Fisher was far the more likely suspect. Aside from his suspicious presence in the village, he had the height, the muscularity and – once I had observed his tattoo – an American connection of the right type. Admittedly, the man whose image I deduced from the scene in Regent's Park, limped. I had not seen Seamus walking, but an examination of his dead body has shown me that he had, indeed, a damaged leg which would have caused a limp.'

He smiled slightly at me, as though he knew the point had worried me, then resumed his narrative.

'It was obvious that, whomsoever the perpetrator might be, they were not going to advertise their guilt. Even when Fisher slew Chater, within yards of our lodgings, he left me with only a strong suspicion. As I told Hopkins and McBrain on their arrival, it was necessary for me to go about my business in such a fashion as to provoke my quarry and draw him out.'

Another sip and on. 'I had already begun to form the theory which I have set out to you this evening about the whereabouts of the gold, and which Inspector McBrain disputes.'

'I do not say you're wrong in your conclusions, Mr Holmes,' interrupted the Scots inspector, 'I was merely observing that your method seems a wee bit fanciful.'

'A wee bit fanciful,' repeated my friend, and for a moment I feared that his tongue might yet break free, but he carried on affably enough.

'Watson here has published the observation that my knowledge of astronomy is lacking. I am not quite the ignoramus that he portrays, but I was aware that it required a more knowledgeable brain than mine to plot the precise passage of the sight line I have described across Inish Beg, so I took the most exact measurements I could, doing so in broad daylight and, to my satisfaction, being observed throughout by somebody with field glasses, whose post of observation was the slope of the hill behind Fisher's lodging.

'My measurements,' he went on, 'I sent, with questions, to Professor Rutledge at the University of Edinburgh. I knew him to be a disciple of Sir Norman Lockyer and an adherent of Lockyer's theories about megalithic stones and their astronomical significances. I also took the opportunity to travel from the village, acquire a few simple properties, and return in the character of Dr Macleod, the American musician.'

'Were you,' said McBrain, 'that Yankee who we met in the inn and who spent so much time with old Breck?' And his face betrayed his astonishment.

'The same,' said Holmes and bowed modestly, deeply gratified, I have no doubt, at having made McBrain feel foolish. 'My change of identity allowed me to become more friendly with Breck, as did my Gaelic pronounced with an American drawl. I tried hard to find in Breck's memory some glimmer of recollection that would point me to the gold, or some observation that would confirm my suspicions of Fisher. I have to admit that my efforts were almost entirely fruitless. The old man seemed utterly bewildered by Chater's death and had no idea of the perpetrator. It was obvious that he could not conceive of his other chum, Fisher, as being the killer. As to the gold, he told me only what he told anyone who asked, that Mungo Breck had left a clue in the painting "Golden Reflections", and recited for me a child's skipping rhyme about the gold. I must observe that, though created after the hiding of the gold, since it refers to the death of Charles Stuart, the rhyme was constructed by someone who knew the gold's location.'

He refilled his glass. 'When it became obvious that I was making no progress with Breck, I staged my "return" to the village and pursued my search for the gold. Professor Rutledge had provided me with diagrams and figures which would enable me to set an exact line on Inish Beg to mark the late-eighteenth-century fall of the sunset alignment.

'I also had to apply myself to the question of our host's failing health, and was soon able to satisfy myself that Watson had been right in his diagnosis of poisoning and that the source was Seamus Fisher. Armed with that conclusion, I was certain that Fisher was our murderer in every case. He had sought to kill the laird in order to pre-empt any claim by our host to gold found on his land.'

The laird shuddered and refilled his glass, without taking medical advice.

'I continued,' said Holmes, 'my practise of carrying out my measurements in public, so that Watson and I were seen on Inish Beg, laying a sight line according to Professor Rutledge's calculations. I was delighted to note that the line ran exactly and precisely at right angles to the line of gypsy graves, between the third and sixth graves, so that they formed, as I had suspected, the marked position which Mungo Breck had placed along the midsummer line. I was also delighted to note that Fisher not only kept us under observation, but sent Breck across to engage us in idle chit-chat while trying to learn what we were doing.'

He smiled broadly around the table. 'My lure,' he said, 'finally worked, though rather earlier than I expected. On that same night, Fisher, convinced (and rightly) that I now knew the exact position of the gold, sought to forestall me. Ewan Breck's superstitious fear of Inish Beg at night was such that he had to be coerced into cooperating with Chater's pistol. As soon as Lacky told me what was going on, I realized that matters had come to a head. What followed were the events on Inish Beg of which you all now know. Fisher sought to make sense of my markers and the copy of McNair's clue that he had taken from Chater's corpse. The arrival of the inspectors distracted him and he dropped the paper. For the first time, Breck saw the bloody fragment and realized whence it came. He tried to shoot Fisher, but the Irishman grasped him and stabbed him savagely, not with the skean-dhu which he kept in his stocking, but with the knife that he wore in a sheath sewn into his jacket. It was only the skill of Watson that felled him and prevented a gun battle on the island.'

My friend placed both hands on the table. 'Now, Laird, gentlemen, I think that I have set the entire affair out succinctly, apart from one small matter, which I shall deal with very shortly.'

There was a pause, during which the whisky and cigars circulated.

'Well, Mr Holmes,' said the laird, 'you have told us a remarkable tale. Do you really believe that the gold is on Inish Beg?'

'I do, Laird. If I might take possession of your cigar box for a minute or two, I believe that I can clinch my argument.'

He took the box and held it up to us, turning it on his hand.

'When first I saw this lovely object, I believed it to have been made as a toiletry box for a lady, because of its internal mirror, but further reflection, if you will forgive the word, led me to a very different conclusion. It is too heavy for feminine use and the mirror has another purpose.

'Laird,' he requested, turning to our host,

'may we have all the lights extinguished except the small candelabra?'

The laird nodded and Hopkins and Mrs Herd, who had been in attendance at the sideboard, went round and dowsed the lights. Once Hopkins was back in his seat, Holmes folded the plan which he had used across the middle and passed it across to me.

'Hold this up in front of you, Watson,' he said.

When all was in place and everyone in the room silent, he pulled the candelabra nearer towards him and opened the cigar box. As we all fascinated, he began to manoeuvre the box until the mirror caught the candles' light. When it did so he gently turned the box until it threw a slightly distorted rectangle of light on to the back of the plan which I held.

From my position I could not see what caused it, but a gasp of astonishment ran around the table. Craning my neck, without daring to let the paper shift, I saw the cause of the response. Lines of writing had appeared, as if by magic, across the lighted rectangle.

I could not read them upside down, but Guthrie leaned across and read them aloud:

'"From the lone pillar set by men of old,
The evening lights Strathcullar with a

sheen of gold.

The western clouds guild the midsummer
sky
Above the isle where the forgotten lie,
Who still may find glory at their Lord's
behest,
When the immortals sail for the golden
west,
Lighting to all whose eyes can seek and
see,
A golden path to future liberty."

'Well!' exclaimed Guthrie, and sat back in
his chair.

'Do you,' asked Holmes of McBrain, 'still
contend that my results were obtained by
coincidence and that the gold may not be on
Inish Beg?'

'I give you best, Mr Holmes,' said the
inspector. 'That is clearly about the gold,
speaking of a "golden path to future liberty"
which is exactly what the gold was intended
to be.'

'Thank you, Inspector,' said Holmes. He
drew a bloodstained paper from his pocket.
'This is the clue that McNair wrote out,
which he found in this castle, and it matches
that inscription.'

Guthrie had taken the box and was examining it closely, running his fingertips across
the mirror.

'There is no inscription of any kind here,

Mr Holmes. How on earth is it done?'

'Shortly before dinner, Watson had occasion to remind me of Mungo Breck's extreme skill with mirrors, as witnessed by the centrepiece of our drinks tray. It caused me to realize where McNair found his clue. Such mirrors were known to the ancient Chinese. The technique is simple and infallible once you know it. A sheet of metal has an inscription or decoration punched into it with hammer blows. It is then carefully polished to a reflecting finish, abolishing all visible trace of the previous stamping. It can be employed as a mirror, or even decorated with etching by acid. However, the blows of the hammer punches have compressed the metal immediately beneath where they fell, so that the reflective index is different at that point and they will reflect at a different angle. Even if there is an etched pattern overlaid, the original stamped pattern will show through when light is reflected from it.'

'Astonishing!' was heard from several mouths, and each diner had to take the box and run his fingertips across the mirror as Guthrie had done.

'You seem to have proved your argument, Mr Holmes,' said Hopkins, 'but why didn't Burgoyne's men look more closely at Inish Beg?'

'Burgoyne's men,' said Holmes, 'will have been mainly Scots, if not Highlanders. They will have had the same superstitious fear of the dead, particularly the dead buried in unhallowed ground, as we see today. What is more, they will have been told that the gypsy graves contained people who died of a nameless infection. If Burgoyne himself had ordered the excavation of those graves there would have been a mutiny among his men and probably a riot among the villagers, in both cases for the fear of infection.'

'But you do not predict any problem with infection now?' asked McBrain.

'No, Inspector. In fact, I predict that no bodies will be found beneath those mounds, only the gold. I suspect that the story of the deaths by disease is another invention of Mungo Breck's, created to keep people away from the gold.'

'Mr Holmes,' said the laird, 'I had no idea that you were going to end your narrative with a magic lantern show. I have rarely, if ever, been so rapt at any table, let alone my own. Mrs Herd, please restore the lamps, we must drink a toast on this.'

So we did, after which our host asked Holmes, 'What, in heaven's name, shall I do about the gold?'

Holmes smiled. 'I am no treasure trove expert,' he said, 'but I believe that you may have a claim on it.'

The laird shook his head vigorously, and Holmes went on, 'Alternatively, I suggest that you wait until you are contacted by the American and British authorities – which will certainly happen once I have made my report. They, and perhaps even the French, will need to decide whose it is if you lay no claim.'

The President's Pleasure

Holmes and I left Strathcullar on the morning of Ewan Breck's funeral. As we stood waiting to board the trap for the station, Lacky's boat pulled slowly away from Inish Mor, carrying the laird, Mrs Herd and young Jessie, all in mourning, as well as Breck's coffin draped in a Stuart banner. A lone piper sounded a lament from the kirkyard, where all of Strathcullar was gathered in mourning, even our landlady, having plied us with shortbread and best wishes to Kirsty Hudson before going to pay her respects.

We doffed our hats until the coffin had been landed and had entered the kirkyard, then took our places aboard our conveyance. As we pulled away, the solemn notes of the pipes followed us all the way up the hillside until we had passed the crest of the eastern pass.

We endured the journey to the railway and the stopping train to Inverness, where at last the comfort of a first class compartment allowed us to relax, and on the following afternoon we reached London.

It was not until the next day that we made an appointment to see the presidential aide in Charing Cross Road.

He smiled at us broadly once we were seated before his desk.

'My word, gentlemen!' he exclaimed. 'You have exceeded my expectations, I confess.'

'Really?' said Holmes.

'I admit,' said the colonel, 'that I instructed you very much as a last desperate attempt to resolve matters. I considered that, if anyone alive could pull it off, it had to be you.'

Holmes inclined his head. 'You are very kind,' he said. 'Nevertheless, I do not believe that I was at my best, and I permitted two more people to die before the resolution, not to mention the attempt to poison the laird. May I ask how you come to know so much about it?'

The colonel grinned widely. 'I admit that I borrowed two officers of our treasury and sent them to Strathcullar. They were instructed entirely to act as a back-up to you gentlemen. They were not to intervene in anything you did unless it became plain that you were in immediate danger. They have wired me a coded outline of your results. As to Chater, he was wanted for murder in the

States. Fisher was known to us while he was in America, but we shall now look into his contacts there.'

'The American holidaymakers!' I exclaimed.

Holmes smiled. 'I have told you often that there are no such things as coincidences, Watson.'

Tea was brought and Holmes embarked upon his report, which consisted of a shortened version of his dissertation at the laird's table.

When he had finished, the colonel rose and shook both of us warmly by the hand.

'I was right,' he said. 'Nobody else could have done it. The president has heard from me by wire and has been kind enough to reply expressing his great pleasure. I'm only sorry that Dr Watson will not be able to turn it all into one of his excellent stories because of the international ramifications.'

'And I,' said my friend, 'am only glad that we do not have to take any part in those exercises.'

In our cab, returning to Baker Street, I asked Holmes if he really thought he had failed to protect Chater and Breck.

'It should not have happened, nor should the laird have come so close to death. I fear that I am growing old, Watson. Perhaps it is time that I found a new interest and left crime to the official police.'

'You would not,' I said, 'have wished to see this late matter left entirely in the hands of Inspector McBrain?'

He smiled. 'Perhaps not,' he said. 'Perhaps not.'

It was a week or two later that a messenger from the presidential aide brought us a letter. It was on the White House's note-paper, with the seal of the United States. From President Theodore Roosevelt, it warmly thanked Holmes and me for our efforts. 'I only wish,' it ended, 'that Dr Watson could embody it in one of those tales which I enjoy so much. Still, once the international ramifications are forgotten your enormous service to the United States may someday be described.'

The international problems were, eventually, solved. The gold was found precisely where Holmes had predicted and another of his predictions was proved true, for there were no burials under the six mounds that bore Mungo Breck's handsome stones. Czernowski-Stuart, according to Holmes, received a fee from the United States on the recovery of the gold, and a second-hand bookshop in London met Holmes' fees in the matter. Holmes recently told me, and I don't know how he knew, that the original gold coins from Inish Beg are still preserved by the United States government in their gold vaults at Fort Knox.

Seamus Fisher, murderer, was buried by the good people of his adopted village on Inish Beg, the island which had so occupied his imagination.

Editor's Notes

As I remarked in the introduction, there is virtually no way in which a manuscript can be proved absolutely to be the work of John H. Watson. No unassailable specimen of Watson's writing has ever been found and the many manuscripts which appear are widely different in appearance. Some are in typescript, some in ink, some in pencil, all on different kinds and sometimes sizes and colours of paper.

As the fact that Holmes and Watson were real people first appeared in print in 1910, one would have hoped that by this time the search of newspapers and official records would have thrown some factual light on their existence and, perhaps, identified the true facts and characters behind the published cases. Alas, Watson seems to have been so skilful at hiding clients' identities that not one case has ever been proven true. He did the same with himself and Sherlock Holmes, to such an extent that no official record of them can be found, apart from what purports to be a photocopy of Watson's military record. Holmes' published essays – on the Motets of Lassus, the Tracing of Footprints, the Varieties of Cigar Ash, Tattoos and other subjects, seem to have vanished without trace.

For these reasons it becomes necessary to see what parts of a Watson narrative may be supported by other sources, and this is the approach which I have adopted. In the notes which follow I have set out the results of my researches into a number of matters mentioned in the text. They do not, I have to tell you, prove that the present narrative is really a previously unpublished account of an inquiry by Sherlock Holmes.

In the end it is for the reader to make up their own mind. All I can do is reiterate that I am as satisfied as reason permits.

Barrie Roberts

Personal Messages

The term 'Jacobite' occurs several times in this narrative. For those who have forgotten their English history, it may help if I add a small explanation.

Henry VIII fell out with the Pope and withdrew the English church from Roman rule, making it an English Catholic church, ruled spiritually and temporally by King Henry who was, as you will recall, a model of spirituality. His daughter, Elizabeth I, made the English church into a Protestant church – the Church of England – and severely persecuted Catholics. This worked well enough until the Stuart family, who already held the throne of Scotland, inherited the English throne. English opinion was very largely against the Stuart family – not because they were Scots, but because they were Catholics. After various irruptions and interruptions, like the execution of one Stuart (Charles I) and the establishment of a commonwealth under a 'Lord Protector', Charles II was invited to come home and all would be forgiven. It was not. Matters came to a head in 1688, when the legitimate King James was forced to flee abroad. His supporters were referred to as 'Jacobites', from the Latinized form of James, Jacobus. Parliament decided that he had abdicated and cast about for a new king. They selected William of Orange, a stoutly Protestant Netherlander, who also happened to be married to a Stuart princess, thereby giving a slight gloss of legality to their games.

The succession to the throne of Britain passed on from William, but in Europe the exiled Stuarts sat about plotting to recover their throne and making mischief. Two particular Stuarts are remembered by history as the 'Old Pretender' and the 'Young Pretender' – James and Charles Stuart respectively. Two major rebellions were launched by the Jacobites in 1715 and 1745, but after a comprehensive defeat at Culloden in 1746, no further attempt was made to restore the Stuart line.

Sherlock Holmes Deduces

The skean-dhu, the 'black knife', is still worn by Scots in full Highland dress and was, as Holmes says, originally a weapon designed for concealment and surprise use

at close quarters. It would be a most difficult weapon to throw with any accuracy, but
I'm sure that with long practise an individual might develop such a skill.

A Plea from America

Who was Czernowski-Stuart? In the nine-
teenth century there were two brothers,
called Sobrieskie-Stuart, who lived in an
islanded castle on a Scottish loch. They
claimed to be the heirs of Bonnie Prince
Charlie and, thereby, heirs to the thrones of
Scotland and England. They were treated by
neighbours and tenants as royalty, though
they passed their time in antiquarian pur-
suits and made no overt claim to the throne.

The problem is that both brothers were
dead before the date of this story and died
without issue. Yet the name of the Laird of
Strathcullar seems to be a Watsonian version
of Sobrieskie-Stuart. Was the laird a nephew
of the two brothers?

There is at present in Scotland a claimant
to the Jacobite succession called Prince
Michael of Albany. He too, so far as I know,
has never made any overt attempt to claim
the British throne.

The presidential aides did exist and, so far
as I know, may still exist. According to infor-

mation published in the States in the 1960s, so far from being personal aides to the president, they were an elite corps of six intelligence officers, one placed in each of six key points around the world, where their business was to keep an eye on matters that might affect the United States in that region. They were, it seems, completely separate from the diplomatic and intelligence services of their country. Congress learned with some alarm at one point that the finance to employ the presidential aides was passed through under a false heading and never succeeded in discovering what that heading was! The novelist Upton Sinclair, in his 'World's End' series of novels, has his hero, Lanning Prescott Budd, appointed as a presidential aide to Franklin D. Roosevelt, though Lanny Budd travels the world and reports in person to the president.

The eighteenth-century American colonists were certainly anxious to sever their ties with King George (or at least, most of them were), but they were not necessarily convinced of the wonder and beauty of a republic. It is a matter of record that approaches were made to George Washington to become 'King of America'. Washington refused them, at least twice. Whether there really was an offer made to Charles James Stuart

I cannot say. It is not an invention of Watson's. The story appears in Lawrence Gardner's *Blood Lines of the Holy Grail* and elsewhere.

References to the United States Treasury are not because the subject is missing gold, but because the United States secret service was, originally, an arm of the Treasury, concerned with the prevention of counterfeiting.

A Reconnaissance

Like the identity of Czernowski-Stuart, the village of Strathcullar poses a problem.

There is, of course, no such place, and we are left to wonder how much of the facts Watson has concealed or altered in his references to the village.

He describes a Highland village, some distance from a railhead, even in those days, set around a large loch. The loch is fed by a river, which enters the valley from a waterfall in the hills to the east. Apart from a number of crannogs around the edges of the loch, there are two larger islands, one with a castle and one with an ancient graveyard. On the eastern approach road is a large megalith, and the remains of a smaller one at the western end of the loch. The village lies along the southern shore of the loch.

Crannogs are as described in Watson's text and were small island fortresses, constructed by heaping stones into a lake, some way from the shore, and laying down a timber floor on which a highly-defensible family home could be constructed.

If Watson's description of 'Strathcullar' were exactly true, it would be the easiest thing in the world to identify it from an Ordnance Survey map. It isn't. There is no village in Scotland which exactly matches Watson's description.

It occurs to me that a clue to the real 'Strathcullar' may be found in the houses of the village. Although Watson does not describe them in detail, it seems that the row of cottages and the inn were rather more spacious than was usual in the dwellings of Highland Scots peasantry a century ago, presumably because Czernowski-Stuart was a caring landlord. An architectural historian might be able to locate the place.

Dinner at Strathcullar Castle

The device which the laird shows Holmes and Watson, of transparent horn discs which each bear part of a figure and can be assembled to resemble one person in particular, was used by Catholics under the Elizabethan persecution. I had not previously heard of them being employed in the Jacobite cause, but they may well have been. After all, the Jacobites were Catholics.

The story of the nine of diamonds is still well known in Scotland, and the card is often nicknamed the 'Curse of Scotland'. It is, of course, a wonderful propaganda story. Working in Scotland forty years ago, I visited Blair Castle in Perthshire and examined the collections there of porcelain, armour, weapons etc. Among the exhibits was an eighteenth-century playing card with the order scribbled on it, which purported to be the original 'Curse of Scotland'. Whether this is the one which Czernowski-Stuart showed to Holmes and Watson sixty years before, I cannot say.

Prince Charlie's Angels

The remarkable tray with a centrepiece that reflected Bonnie Prince Charlie's portrait is not an invention. There really were such devices, and at least one has survived into modern times. There can never have been many of them, in view of the extreme patience and skill that it must have taken to construct them.

The artist and craftsman Mungo Breck seems as unknown to the art world today as he was in 1902, and the whereabouts of his painting 'Golden Reflections' is unknown. It has not passed through any auction house in the last century, though I suppose it might still be in private hands. Perhaps it will turn up on the 'Antiques Roadshow' one day!

Danger in the Dark

When Watson refers to his own injuries, it is often difficult to be sure whether he means the wounds that invalided him out of the Army or something more recent.

Here he makes reference to an injury that made it difficult for him to keep his balance in a small boat, which suggests the lameness that plagued him after his return from Afghanistan. However, earlier in the year of this narrative he had taken a bullet graze and, in the manuscript which I edited as *Sherlock Holmes and the Harvest of Death*, he complains that in hot weather the recent injury caused him irritation.

As to his military wounds, most commentators agree that he was wounded at least twice in Afghanistan, once in the subclavian artery (which he specified) and once in a leg or thigh which caused the lameness.

I am intrigued by Holmes' reference to a Welshman who appeared at Hyde Park Corner telling the crowds that he was the last legitimate Tudor and, thereby, the true monarch of Britain. There was such a man that I recall from the late 1950s, but he was too young to have been the speaker to whom Holmes refers. Perhaps it was a lineal ancestor.

The Island of the Outcast Dead

After some five centuries of moving east from their original home in India, the Romani gypsies reached Britain in Tudor times. They were widely believed to have come from Egypt, and the first laws against them refer to them as Egyptians, hence the nickname 'gypsies'. The non-Romani travellers, who were already here when the Romanis arrived and whose language, Shelta, is completely distinct from the Sanskrit-descended Romani, are known in Scotland as 'tinkers' or 'tinklers'. They prefer to be known merely as 'travellers'.

The Official Police

Holmes' comments on how Watson's stories

had made him universally recognizable may have been intended as a jibe at Watson, but it actually serves as a tribute to the accuracy of Sidney Paget's illustrations to Watson's stories. At least we can be reasonably sure of the Great Detective's appearance, if almost nothing else!

Note that Holmes refers to John Wilkes Booth as the 'alleged' assassin of President Lincoln. By the period of this narrative, Holmes and Watson had met Booth – had indeed taken him as a client – and confirmed what many people believed and believe: that the murder of Lincoln was a great deal more complicated a matter than the farcical trial of the alleged co-conspirators suggested and that Booth survived into old age. See my edited publication *Sherlock Holmes and the Royal Flush*, Constable & Co.

McNair's Clue

The use of cigarette ash brushed lightly across a paper with the intention of bringing up the image of anything written on a sheet above which had left an impression, seems to have been a bit of a speciality of Sherlock Holmes. It does work, and I know it was used by some American police forces in the 1940s. Nowadays the technique is called electronic static dispersal analysis and is carried out with the aid of expensive machines.

Watson's comment on 'Gentlemanly Johnny' Burgoyne may have irritated Holmes, but was fair. Playing a prominent part in the campaign against the American rebels, Burgoyne was forced into a humiliating surrender at Saratoga. Theatregoers may recall him as a character in Shaw's *The Devil's Disciple*, and movie buffs will recall Sir Laurence Olivier playing him opposite Kirk Douglas in the film version.

Holmes' Observations

Holmes never offered Watson his theories on the broken Pictish stone at the western end of the loch. The crudely carved Celtic cross is, as Holmes did mention, probably evidence of a Christian attempt to remove the pagan influence, but the smashing of the stone is more interesting. Was it deliberately broken by Mungo Breck to avoid drawing too much attention to his clues?

The boxwood instrument which Watson did not recognize was, most probably, an inclinometer.

A Visit from the Doctor

The symptoms which Watson noted in the laird appear to be those of Vitamin A poisoning; certainly the hair loss is.

The Phantom of Inish Beg

The practise of 'waking' the newly departed is strongly rooted in Celtic tradition, particularly in Ireland.

It derives from the belief that the soul does not leave the body until the corpse is properly interred. Consequently, it is necessary to maintain a watch (or wake) over the dead, to prevent the devil stealing their souls if they are left unguarded. In some parts of rural Ireland and Wales a 'sin-eater' would be invited to eat a meal from a plate placed on the corpse's chest, thereby, it was believed, absorbing the deceased's sins. It can be imagined that only the poorest and most wretched would perform this ritual for a free meal.

Many primitive peoples have believed that the soul is not free of the body until the flesh has disappeared. In parts of Greece, they used to exhume the dead at intervals, to see if there was any flesh remaining. When only a skeleton remained it was time to move it to a permanent tomb.

The Return of Sherlock Holmes

There are still (I hope) wildcats in the more remote parts of Scotland, as opposed to domestic cats gone wild. The native wildcat is not a creature one should tangle with thoughtlessly.

Resurrection Men

I am aware that dog liver is poisonous to humans, though I was not aware that this was known to the Esquimaux a century ago. It seems that dogs are unable to eliminate Vitamin A from their system, so that it builds up in their livers and is passed on to anyone unwise enough to eat them, causing serious, and sometimes fatal, illness. The older the dog, the greater the accumulation.

While I recognize Holmes' extraordinary knowledge of poisons, I would love to know how he came to know about Vitamin A poisoning from dogs' livers.

Some years after the date of the present story, in 1908, an expedition led by Sir Douglas Mawson raised the Union flag over the South Geographic Pole. Returning later from the Australian Antarctic Expedition, Mawson's party lost the sledge carrying the bulk of their supplies down a crevasse.

The journey home was a dreadful one, in the course of which they were forced to kill and eat their huskies. One of Mawson's companions died, almost certainly of Vitamin A poisoning.

To Inish Beg Again

The tune 'For He's a Jolly Good Fellow' was certainly about in the eighteenth century. A version of it carried the lyric 'Marlborough has gone to War'. In America, apart from the popular, congratulatory lyric, it is also known as 'A Bear Climbed Over a Mountain' and 'Molly Brooks Has Gone to War' (a corruption of the 'Marlborough' version).

Interestingly, in view of the content of the Strathcullar skipping song, the European gypsies have a Romani version of the Marlborough song to much the same tune.

Sherlock Holmes Explains

It is true that the name 'whisky' comes from the Gaelic *'usque baugh'* and means 'the water of life'.

How Sherlock Holmes Did It

It was, I believe, Sir Norman Lockyer who first showed some of the sun alignments from Stonehenge. When Gerald Hawkins demonstrated others in the 1960s, the British archaeological establishment was not inclined to accept his findings, but further work by Aubrey Burl and others has shown that many megalithic sites have astrological significance and that some embody lines like that at Strathcullar.

It is true that in British Christian grave-yards the tombstone is traditionally placed at the head of the grave, facing east. Occasionally one can be found reversed. This was a superstitious attempt to stop the spirit of the person beneath from rising. See my *Midland Murders and Mysteries*, Quercus Books, where I recount a true story of a Staffordshire murder victim whose grave-stone was reversed because people feared that his spirit would rise and seek vengeance on his murderer.

The 'magic mirror' demonstrated by Holmes was, indeed, known to the Chinese long ago, and was made by the technique he outlines. A variation of the technique has been used for some years to catch car thieves. If thieves grind away the engine-block registration number of a car and place a spurious one on top of it, the original number is discovered by grinding away the new number and slanting a beam of light across the surface. The legitimate number will be revealed and can be photographed.

The President's Pleasure

I have been unable to find any record of the shipment of Bonnie Prince Charlie's gold, its hiding or its rediscovery. Nevertheless, the French did assist anyone who embarrassed their English enemy. They certainly contributed gold to the 1715 and 1745 Jacobite rebellions. One such French hoard is believed to lie still hidden, somewhere near Rannoch Moor.

It would be no great surprise if the original Strathcullar coins do still lie in Fort Knox. After all, it is persistently rumoured that the gold bars which Britain paid to the United States in the 'Alabama' dispute, after the American Civil War, are still untouched in Fort Knox's vaults

Was this the case that convinced the Great Detective into retiring? (See Sherlock Holmes' further comments on retirement in *Sherlock Holmes and the Harvest of Death*, which I edited for Constable & Co and which follows chronologically on from the present narrative.) Certainly he had gone by the autumn of the following year, despite occasional reappearances.

An interesting question arises as to who inherited Holmes' papers. Various biographers have stated that Watson died well before Holmes (though nobody can produce a reliable date for either death). When did Mycroft Holmes die? Did he inherit his younger brother's estate? How much of the contents of 221b did Holmes take with him into retirement in Sussex? What became of the contents of his retirement home? At least one account says that Watson shared the house with Holmes in the 1940s, though another says that Watson died in 1928. Is the whole collection from Baker Street still intact somewhere – including the Stradivarius, the experimental equipment, the Persian slipper and such trifles as a letter to Sherlock from President Theodore Roosevelt?

If any piece of genuine Holmes memorabilia turns up on the 'Antiques Roadshow' or 'Flog It!', perhaps produced by some connection of the good Mrs Hudson, I hope I shall be around to see the valuer's face!